PENGUIN BOOKS

THOSE WITHOUT SHADOWS

Françoise Sagan was born in 1935. Her father is a prosperous Paris industrialist whose family were originally Spanish. She took her *nom de plume* from the Princess de Sagan of Marcel Proust. She was eighteen years old when she wrote her best-selling *Bonjour Tristesse*. She had failed to pass her examinations at the Sorbonne and she decided to write a novel. The book received great acclaim in France, where in 1959 it had sold 850,000 copies, and also abroad. Her second and third books, *A Certain Smile* and *Those Without Shadows*, have also had tremendous popularity in France, Great Britain, and the U.S.A. Her fourth book, *Aimez-vous Brahms . . .*, appeared in 1959 and *Wonderful Clouds* in 1961. Since then she has published *La Chamade* (1965), *The Heart-Keeper* (1968), *Sunlight on Cold Water* (1971), *Scars on the Soul* (1974) and *Lost Profile* (1976), as well as two plays, *Un piano dans l'herbe* (1970) and *Zaphorie* (1973).

Françoise Sagan is married and has a son.

FRANÇOISE SAGAN

THOSE WITHOUT
SHADOWS

TRANSLATED BY
IRENE ASH

PENGUIN BOOKS

Penguin Books Ltd, Harmondsworth, Middlesex, England
Penguin Books, 625 Madison Avenue, New York, New York 10022, U.S.A.
Penguin Books Australia Ltd, Ringwood, Victoria, Australia
Penguin Books Canada Ltd, 2801 John Street, Markham, Ontario, Canada L3R 1B4
Penguin Books (N.Z.) Ltd, 182–190 Wairau Road, Auckland 10, New Zealand

—

Dans un mois, dans un an first published 1957
This translation first published by John Murray 1957
Published in Penguin Books 1961
Reprinted 1964, 1966, 1973, 1978

—

Copyright © Françoise Sagan, 1957
All rights reserved

—

Made and printed in Great Britain
by Cox & Wyman Ltd,
London, Reading and Fakenham
Set in Monotype Bembo

TO GUY SCHÖLLER

These deeds must not be thought after these ways; so, it will make us mad. MACBETH, Act II, Sc. I

ONE

BERNARD entered the café, hesitated a moment under the inquiring glances of the few customers seated beneath the disfiguring neon lights, and hastened towards the cashier. He always liked cashiers, buxom, respectable women, following their own thoughts, interrupted only by the clink of money and the striking of matches. Unsmiling, and with a look of boredom, she handed him a coin. It was nearly four in the morning. The telephone box was dirty, the receiver damp. He dialled Josée's number. He had been walking across Paris all night so as to tire himself sufficiently to telephone to her without emotion. Anyhow, there was not much sense in ringing up a girl at such an hour. Naturally she would not refer to his bad manners, but the act itself was suggestive of an *enfant terrible*; and he despised it. He was not in love with Josée, but he wanted to know what she was doing, and all day long had been obsessed by this thought. The telephone rang and a man's sleepy voice said 'Hallo', then almost at once Josée asked: 'Who's there?'

7

Bernard did not move, petrified with fear in case she should guess who it was, and afraid of being suspected of spying on her. It was an awful moment. He hung up the receiver and lit a cigarette. Soon he was walking along the quayside swearing to himself. At the same time an inner voice told him that Josée had no obligation towards him; she was rich and free and he was not even her recognized lover. But he already realized that the torment which had driven him towards the telephone would continue to be his strongest feeling for some time to come. He had acted the young man of the world, talked about life and books in a detached manner, and spent a night with her, and it had to be admitted Josée's was the kind of flat that made this easy.

Now he was going home to find his bad novel lying in disorder on his desk, and his wife in bed asleep. She was always asleep at that hour, her fair, childish face turned towards the door as if she feared he would never come back, awaiting him anxiously in her sleep as she had done all day.

The young man put down the receiver, and Josée controlled the anger she had felt when she saw him take it up and answer as if he were in his own home.

8

'I don't know who it was,' he said sulkily, 'he rang off.'

'Why do you say "he"?' asked Josée.

'It is always a man who telephones to a woman in the middle of the night and then rings off,' said the young man, yawning.

She looked at him with curiosity, wondering why she had allowed him to bring her back after dinner at Alain's and come up with her afterwards. He was quite good-looking, but vulgar and uninteresting. Far less intelligent than Bernard, and in a way less attractive. He sat on the bed and reached for his watch.

'Four o'clock,' he said, 'what a horrible hour!'

'Why do you say that?'

He did not reply, but turned and looked at her fixedly over his shoulder. She returned his look and began to pull the sheet up to cover herself. She knew what he was thinking. He had taken her home, crudely made love, and then fallen asleep beside her. Now he looked calmly at her. He hardly cared what she was and what she thought of him. She belonged to him at this moment and felt neither irritation nor anger at his assurance, but only a deep humility.

He raised his eyes to her face and ordered her to put down the sheet. She did so while he stared at her with deliberation. She felt ashamed and could neither move, nor find the flippant phrase that, as she turned over, she would have used to Bernard, or anyone else. In any case he would not have understood or laughed. She knew that he had a fixed idea of her which he would never change. Her heart was beating fast. She thought, with a feeling of triumph: 'I am lost.' The young man leant towards her, a mysterious smile on his lips. She watched him approach without blinking.

'We may as well make some use of that telephone call,' he said as he fell upon her. She closed her eyes.

'I shall never be able to take this lightly again,' she thought, 'it will never again be something easy, nocturnal; it will always be bound up with that look of his.'

*

'Can't you sleep?'

Fanny Maligrasse groaned:

'It's my asthma. Alain, do be kind, and fetch me a cup of tea.'

Alain Maligrasse slowly got out of bed and carefully put on his dressing-gown. Fanny and Alain had been very happy together for many years, until the war. After four years' separation they had found each other very much changed when they came together again in their fifties. Almost unconsciously they had adopted a touching modesty. Each tried to hide from the other the changes of the passing years. At the same time they had both developed a great liking for the young. People said sympathetically about the Maligrasses that they loved to be surrounded by youth, and for once what they said was true. They loved young people, not just as a distraction, but because they found them more interesting than their own contemporaries. The freshness of youth appealed to them and they took every opportunity of strengthening these friendships.

As Alain put the tray on his wife's bed, he looked at her with compassion. Her small, thin, dark face was tense with insomnia, only her eyes remained unchanged in their beauty, a touching blue-grey, brilliant, and vivacious.

'It was a successful evening, don't you think so?' she said, taking the cup.

Alain looked at her rather wrinkled throat as she drank her tea, but his mind was elsewhere. He made an effort to reply:

'I can't understand why Bernard always comes without his wife,' he said. 'Although one must admit that Josée is very attractive.'

'So is Béatrice,' said Fanny, laughing.

Alain began to laugh too. His admiration for Béatrice was a source of amusement between his wife and himself. But she could not know how painful this joke had become for him. Every week, after their Monday reception, as they jokingly referred to it, he went to bed shivering. Béatrice was beautiful and impetuous; when he thought of her, these two qualifications forced themselves upon his mind and he could repeat them to himself indefinitely. 'Beautiful and impetuous.' Béatrice concealing her dark, tragic face when she laughed, as laughing did not become her; Béatrice talking angrily about her profession because she had not yet had any success; Béatrice being rather silly, as Fanny would say. Silly, yes, she was rather silly, but always with a lyrical note.

Alain had been working in a publishing house for twenty years. He was badly paid, cultured, and very fond of his wife. How had it happened that their joke about Béatrice had become the enormous weight he had to lift every morning when he got up? The weight he dragged about with him every day until Monday came round? For on Mondays Béatrice always came to their 'evenings', and he played the role of an intellectual and charming middle-aged man, witty and absent-minded. He was in love with Béatrice.

'Béatrice hopes to have a small part in X's new play,' said Fanny. 'Were there enough sandwiches?' The Maligrasses were hard put to it to continue entertaining their friends. The fashion of offering whisky at parties had been a catastrophe for them.

'I believe so,' answered Alain. He was sitting on the edge of the bed, his hands dangling between his thin knees. Fanny watched him with tenderness and pity.

'Your little cousin from Normandy arrives tomorrow,' she said. 'I hope he has a pure heart and noble soul, and that Josée will fall in love with him.'

'Josée never falls in love with anyone. Shall we try to get some sleep?'

He took the tray from his wife's knees, kissed her forehead and cheek, and lay down. He felt cold in spite of the radiator. He was an old man and he was cold. And all the literature in the world could not help him.

*

Dans un mois, dans un an, comment souffrirons-nous,
Seigneur, que tant de mers me séparent de vous
Que le jour recommence et que le jour finisse
Sans que jamais Titus puisse voir Bérénice.

Béatrice stood in her dressing-gown gazing at herself in front of the mirror. The verses fell from her lips like stone flowers. 'Where did I read that?' she thought, and she felt infinitely sad. At the same time she was angry. For the past five years she had been reciting Bérénice, first for her ex-husband, and lately for her mirror. She wished she were in front of the dark foaming sea of a theatre auditorium, even if there had been nothing more for her to say than: 'Dinner is served, Madame.'

'I'd do anything for that,' she confided to her reflection, and her reflection smiled at her.

*

As for the cousin from Normandy, young Édouard Maligrasse; at that moment he was getting into the train which was to take him to the capital.

TWO

BERNARD rose from his chair for the tenth time that morning, went over to the window, and leant against it. He could not bear it any more. Writing humiliated him. What he wrote humiliated him. As he read through his last pages he had a feeling of utter futility. The words contained nothing that he wished to say, none of the essential truths that he sometimes thought he perceived. Bernard earned his living by writing for newspapers and magazines, and was a reader in the firm where Alain worked. He had published a novel three years earlier which was said by the critics to possess a 'certain psychological quality'. He had two desires: to write a good novel and, more recently, to possess Josée. But the right words continued to elude him, and Josée had disappeared, carried away by one of those sudden infatuations for a country or for a young man (one could never tell which) that her father's fortune and her charm permitted her to indulge in on the spur of the moment.

'What's the matter?'

Nicole was standing behind him. He had asked her not to disturb him at work, but she could not resist coming into his study with the excuse that she only saw him in the mornings. He would not admit it, but he was aware that she could not live without him. After three years she loved him more every day, and this, he felt, was almost repulsive, for she no longer attracted him. He liked to re-member the picture of himself when they had been in love, the decision he had shown in marrying her, for since that time he had never been able to make any decision at all.

'I'm afraid it's not going very well. After such a bad start there seems little hope.'

'Oh, I'm sure you're mistaken.'

Her tender optimism annoyed him more than anything. If Josée or Alain had said the same thing, it might have given him some comfort. But Josée admitted that she knew nothing about writing, and Alain, though he was encouraging, put on a show of modesty. 'The essential thing is what one discovers afterwards,' he would say. What did he mean? Bernard pretended to understand, but all that jargon annoyed him. 'Writing is just having a sheet of paper, a pen, and not the shadow of an idea what you're going to say,' said Fanny. He liked Fanny very much. He liked them all. He loved nobody. Josée irritated him. He needed her, that was all; and it made him feel suicidal.

Nicole was still there. She was tidying the room; she spent her time tidying up the small flat where he left her alone all day. She knew neither Paris nor literature; both aroused her admiration and her fear. Her only clue might have been Bernard, who eluded her. He was more intelligent than she was, and more attractive. People ran after him. At the moment she could not have children. She only knew Rouen and her father's chemist's shop. One day Bernard had told her this, and afterwards begged her to forgive him. At such times he was as weak as a child, almost in tears. But she preferred these sudden attacks of cruelty to the continuous cruelty of his leaving her after lunch every day with an absent-minded kiss, and only coming back late at night. Bernard and his worries had always been a heaven-sent gift to her. But marriage does not consist only of such gifts. He looked at her; she was rather pretty and rather sad.

'Would you like to come to the Maligrasses' with me this evening?' he asked kindly.

'I would like to very much,' she said.

Suddenly she looked happy, and Bernard felt remorseful, but his remorse was so old and worn out that it never lasted long. He risked nothing by taking her. Josée would not be there. She would have ignored him if he had come with his wife, or she would only have talked to Nicole. She had a way of pretending to be kind which she knew was sometimes useful.

'I'll come and fetch you about nine o'clock,' he said. 'What are you doing today?' Then he added quickly, as he knew she had nothing to answer: 'Try to read this manuscript for me will you? I shall never find the time.' He knew very well that it was useless. Nicole had so much respect for the written word, such admiration for the work of others, however inept, that she was incapable of any critical judgement. Yet she would feel obliged to read it, hoping perhaps to be of some use to him. 'She'd like to be indispensable,' he thought angrily as he went down the stairs, 'what fools women are!' When he reached the entrance he saw his angry expression in the mirror and felt ashamed. It was all a ghastly muddle.

On his arrival at the office he found Alain very excited:

'Béatrice has just telephoned. She asked you to ring her back at once.'

Just after the war Bernard had had a rather tempestuous affair with Béatrice. Now there was a condescending kindness in his attitude towards her which obviously disconcerted Alain.

'Bernard?' (Béatrice was using the solemn voice reserved for important occasions). 'Bernard, do you know X? Don't you publish his plays?'

'I know him slightly,' said Bernard.

'Fanny heard him mention my name in connexion with his new play. I simply must meet him and talk to him. Do this for me, please, Bernard.'

There was something in her voice that reminded Bernard of the best days of their youth after the war, when they had both left a comfortable home and come together, neither of them knowing where their next meal would come from. Béatrice had once persuaded the owner of a bar, well-known for his meanness, to lend them a thousand francs just with that voice of hers. Such power of personality was probably rare nowadays.

'I'll arrange it. I will ring you up this evening.'

'At five o'clock,' said Béatrice firmly. 'Bernard, I love you, I've always loved you.'

'Two years,' said Bernard, laughing.

Still laughing, he turned to Alain and saw his expression. He looked away at once. Béatrice's voice could be heard all over the room.

'Good. In any case I shall see you this evening at Alain's?'

'Yes, of course.'

'He is beside me, do you want to talk to him?' said Bernard. (He did not know why he asked the question.)

'No, I have no time. Give him my love.'

Maligrasse's hand was already reaching towards the receiver. Bernard who had his back to him could only see the well-kept hand with its swollen veins.

'I'll tell him,' he said. 'Good-bye.'

The hand fell. Bernard waited a moment before turning round.

'She sends you her love,' he said at last. 'She has someone waiting for her.'

Bernard felt very unhappy.

*

Josée pulled up her car in front of the Maligrasses' house in the rue de Tournon. The lamplight gleamed on the dusty hood and the mosquitoes stuck to the windscreen.

'I'm definitely not going with you,' said Jacques. 'I should not know what to say to them. I shall work instead.'

Josée felt both relieved and disappointed. The past week with him in the country had been rather overwhelming. He was either stubbornly silent or extremely noisy. Both these moods had ended by frightening as much as they attracted her.

'When I've done some work, I'll drop in and see you,' said the young man. 'Try not to be back too late.'

'I don't know whether I shall come back at all,' said Josée crossly.

'Very well then, just tell me,' he answered. 'It's not worth my coming for nothing. I haven't got a car.'

She did not know what he was thinking. She put her hand on his shoulder:

'Jacques,' she said.

He looked at her calmly. She stroked his face and he frowned:

'Do you like me?' he said with a slight laugh.

It's funny, he must think I can't do without him, or something of that sort. Jacques F., medical student, my hero. It is really quite amusing. It's not even a question of physical attraction. I don't know if it is the reflection of myself in him that I like, or the absence of that reflection, or just him himself. But he is not interesting, he is probably not even cruel. He just exists, that is the word for it.

'I quite like you,' she said seriously, 'but, so far, it is not a great passion.'

'Great passion exists.'

'Heavens!' thought Josée, 'he must be in love with some ethereal, fair-haired young girl. Could I be jealous of her?'

'Have you ever felt a great passion for anyone?' she asked.

'No, but a friend of mine has.'

She burst out laughing, he looked at her wondering whether he ought to be angry, then laughed too. His laughter was not gay, but raucous, almost angry.

Béatrice made a triumphal entry at the Maligrasses' and even Fanny was struck by her beauty. Nothing suits certain women better than ambition. Love makes them ugly. Alain Maligrasse rushed to meet her and kissed her hand.

'Is Bernard here?' she asked.

She looked for him among the dozen or so people who had already arrived, and would have trampled Alain under foot to get to Bernard. Alain moved aside, his face devastated by the sudden disappointment. Bernard was sitting on a sofa near his wife and an unknown young man. In spite of her haste, Béatrice recognized Nicole and was seized with pity for her. She was sitting upright, her hands on her knees and a timid smile on her face. 'I must teach her how to live,' thought Béatrice with a feeling she took to be kindness.

'Bernard,' she said, 'you are really an awful person. Why didn't you ring me up at five o'clock? I phoned you a dozen times at the office. How do you do, Nicole.'

'I went to see X,' said Bernard triumphantly. 'We are all three meeting for a drink at six tomorrow.'

Béatrice let herself drop on to the sofa, brushing against the unknown young man. She apologized. Fanny came up to them:

'Béatrice, I don't think you know Alain's cousin, Édouard Maligrasse?'

She noticed him and smiled. He had something irresistible about him, an air of youth and surprising goodness. He looked at her with such astonishment that she began to laugh and Bernard joined in.

'What's the matter? Is my hair untidy, or do I look mad?'

Béatrice liked people to think her mad. But now she was well aware that the young man thought her beautiful.

'You don't look at all mad,' he said. 'I'm sorry if you imagined . . .'

He seemed so discomfited that she turned

away in embarrassment. Bernard looked at her, smiling. The young man got up and walked rather uncertainly towards the table in the dining-room.

'He's crazy about you,' said Bernard.

'Listen, it is you who are crazy. I've only just arrived.' But she was already prepared to believe it. She liked to think that people were crazy about her, although it did not make her feel particularly proud.

'It is supposed only to happen in novels, but he's a romantic young man,' said Bernard, 'he has just come from the provinces to live in Paris, he has never been in love and admits it despairingly. But the cause of his despair will soon change. Our beautiful Béatrice is going to make him suffer.'

'I'd rather you talked to me about X,' said Béatrice. 'Is he a homosexual?'

'Béatrice, you really want to know too much,' said Bernard.

'It isn't that,' said Béatrice, 'but I don't get on with homosexuals. They bore me. I only like normal people.'

'I don't know any homosexuals,' said Nicole.

'That doesn't matter,' said Bernard, 'in any case there are three here. . . .'

But he stopped suddenly. Josée had just arrived. She was laughing with Alain in the doorway and

24

at the same time glancing into the room. She looked tired and had a black smudge on her cheek. She did not see him. Bernard felt a dull pain.

'Josée, where have you been?' exclaimed Béatrice. Josée turned, saw them, and came across the room almost without smiling. She looked exhausted and happy. At twenty-five, she still had an air of adolescence which made her resemble Bernard.

He got up.

'I don't think you know my wife,' he said, 'Josée Saint-Gilles.' Josée smiled without blinking. She kissed Béatrice and sat down. Bernard stood in front of them. His one thought was 'If only she had no money! Where has she come from? What has she been doing for the past ten days?'

'I've been to the country for ten days,' she said, 'the leaves are all russet-coloured.'

'You look tired,' said Bernard.

'I would like to go to the country,' said Nicole. She looked at Josée with sympathy, she was the first person who had not intimidated her. Josée was only frightening when one knew her well, then her amiability became deadly.

'Do you like the country?' said Josée.

'There we go,' thought Bernard furiously, 'now she's going to take an interest in Nicole and talk to her. Do you like the country? Poor Nicole, she already sees herself as her friend.' He went over to the bar, making up his mind to get drunk.

Nicole's eyes followed him. Josée saw the look with a mixture of irritation and pity. She had taken a certain interest in Bernard, but he had soon proved to be too like herself, too unstable, for her to become attached to him. And evidently he had felt the same. She tried to answer Nicole, but felt bored. She was tired of all these people, who appeared to her lifeless. Her holiday had lasted a long time, she seemed to have returned from an endless journey to an unreal country.

'. . . and as I don't know anyone who has a car,' Nicole was saying, 'I can never go for a walk in the woods.' She stopped and added suddenly: 'Nor anyone who hasn't a car either.' The bitterness in her words struck Josée.

'Are you lonely?' she asked.

But Nicole was already frightened of having said too much:

'No, no, I didn't mean it, and besides, I like the Maligrasses.'

Josée hesitated for a moment. Three years before, she would have questioned her, tried to help, but she was tired. Tired of herself and her life. What did that crude young man Jacques or this drawing-room really mean to her? She already knew she must not seek the answer to these questions, as there was no answer.

'If you like, the next time I go for a drive, I'll come and fetch you,' she said to Nicole.

Bernard had achieved his wish: he was slightly drunk, and therefore found young Maligrasse's conversation delightful, although at any other time it would have annoyed him.

'You say she's called Béatrice? She is on the stage? Where? I'll go tomorrow. You see, it's most important for me to get to know her well. I've written a play and I think she would be just right for the heroine.'

Édouard Maligrasse spoke with enthusiasm. Bernard began to laugh: 'You haven't written any play. You're simply falling in love with Béatrice. You are going to suffer, my friend. Béatrice is sweet, but she's all ambition.'

'Bernard, don't talk disparagingly of Béatrice. She adores you this evening,' interrupted Fanny. 'And besides I want you to hear that young man play.'

She indicated a young man who was going towards the piano. Bernard went to sit at Josée's feet. He felt tremendously free and lighthearted.

'My dear Josée,' he would say, 'it's a great

nuisance, but I am in love with you,' and it would probably be true. He suddenly remembered the way she had put her arms round his neck the first time he had kissed her, in the library at her flat, the way she had nestled against him, and how the blood had rushed to his heart. Surely she must love him!

The pianist was playing music that seemed to him tender and lovely, with a certain phrase that was always being repeated, like music with a bowed head. Bernard suddenly understood what he must write, and how he must develop his theme; that phrase was the Josée in every man's imagination, his youth and melancholy desires. 'Ah!' he thought exaltedly, 'that is *the little phrase*! Ah! Proust! But that is Proust, and after all what have I to do with him?' He took Josée's hand, but she drew it away. Nicole looked at him and he smiled because he was fond of her.

*

Édouard Maligrasse was a young man with a pure heart. He did not confuse vanity with love; he had no other ambition than to have a great passion. From the emptiness of life in Caen he arrived in Paris like an unarmed conqueror, with no particular wish to succeed, to have a sports car, or to impress anyone. His father had found him a modest position in an insurance agency which he had enjoyed very much for a week. He liked omnibuses, café counters, and the smiles women gave him; for there was something very charming about him: it was not merely his innocence, but a certain ardour.

Béatrice inspired in him an immediate passion, and above all a violent desire, which the wife of the lawyer in Caen, his former mistress, had never done. She had entered the Maligrasses' drawing-room enhanced by the glamour of a free and easy manner, elegance, the theatre, and heightened by ambition, a quality that he admired though he did not understand it. But a day would come when Béatrice would say to him as her head fell back before his embrace: 'You are more important to me than my career,' and he would bury his face in her black hair, would kiss that tragic mask, would force her to keep silent. He was telling himself all this as he drank his lemonade while the young man played the piano. He liked Bernard, he saw in him that mixture of irony and eagerness so suited to a Parisian journalist, which Balzac had described.

He rushed forward to escort Béatrice home, but she had a small car lent her by a friend, and she offered to drop him.

'I could go with you and then walk back,' he said.

But she insisted that it was unnecessary. So she left him at the corner of boulevard Haussmann and the rue Tronchet, not far from his room. He looked so forlorn that she put her hand up to his cheek and said 'Good-bye, you goat,' for it amused her to find animal resemblances in people. Moreover this goat seemed about to go quietly into the pen, which at this moment was by chance empty of admirers. He was really quite good-looking, she thought. And there he still stood, as if bewitched by the hand that she had put out of the door. He was panting a little like an animal at bay, and she felt a moment of emotion which made her give him her telephone number sooner than she usually did. From then on the exchange 'Élysées' became the symbol of life and progress for Édouard. He walked across Paris with winged feet like all young people in love. Meanwhile Béatrice recited Phèdre in front of her mirror. It was very good practice. Above all success demanded discipline and hard work, no one knew that better than she.

THREE

THE first meeting between Jacques and those whom Josée for nearly a month had secretly called 'the others' was a failure. She had kept him from them because she knew they would not accept him. This often made her feel tempted to break away from them. The bond between Josée and 'the others' was based on good taste, a certain esteem, and on manners, which Jacques did not possess. Fanny was the only one who might perhaps understand and it was with her that Josée began her tour of introductions.

She had gone to tea with Fanny at the rue de Tournon; Jacques was to come and fetch her. He had told her that his presence at the Maligrasses' the evening they met had come about by chance: he had been taken there by one of Béatrice's admirers. 'And you might quite easily have missed me because I was bored stiff and just leaving,' he told her. She had not asked him why he did not say 'I might have missed you,' or 'We might have missed each other.' He always spoke of his relations with other people as an accident that had happened to them, without specifying whether it was an unfortunate one. Josée ended by thinking it was not, that he himself was obviously the accident and that she was already getting tired of it. However, neither annoyance nor her boredom was strong enough as yet to outweigh her curiosity about him.

Fanny was alone at home reading a new novel. She read all the new novels but never quoted anything but Flaubert or Rousseau, knowing that with them she would never fail to be striking. She and Josée were fond of each other, although at times they had misunderstandings. There was a mutual deep-seated confidence between them which perhaps neither felt towards anyone else. They talked first about Édouard's mad passion for Béatrice and of the part Béatrice had obtained in X's play.

'She'll act better in X's play than she will towards poor Édouard,' said Fanny.

Fanny was tiny, her hair was beautifully done, and her movements were graceful. The mauve sofa and her English furniture formed a good background for her.

'You and your flat suit each other, Fanny; and I think that's rare.'

'Who decorated yours?' inquired Fanny. 'Oh,

yes, it was Levègue, of course. It has turned out well, hasn't it?'

'I don't know,' said Josée. 'People tell me so. I don't really think it suits me, besides I never have the feeling that my surroundings suit me, but sometimes people do.'

She thought of Jacques and blushed. Fanny looked at her.

'You're blushing. I think you have too much money, Josée. What about your lectures at the École du Louvre? And how are your parents?'

'You know that the École du Louvre means nothing to me. My parents are still in North Africa. They just send me cheques. I am still absolutely useless in the world. I don't really care, but . . .' She hesitated: 'I want desperately to do something that I would enjoy passionately. What a lot of passion in one sentence!'

She stopped and said quickly:

'And you?'

'I?'

Fanny Maligrasse opened her eyes wide with an amused look.

'Yes, you're always the one who listens. Let's change roles. Am I being indiscreet?'

'No,' said Fanny, laughing, 'but I have Alain.'

Josée raised her eyebrows; there was a silence

while they looked at each other as if they were the same age.

'Is it as obvious as all that?' asked Fanny.

There was something in her voice which touched Josée and embarrassed her. Fanny got up and began to walk about the room.

'I don't know what there is about Béatrice. Her beauty? Or that blind force? She's the only one among us who really has ambition.'

'And Bernard?'

'Bernard loves literature more than anything else. It is not the same thing. And then he's intelligent. There are advantages in some kinds of stupidity.'

She thought again of Jacques and decided to speak to Fanny about him; she had previously made up her mind just to let him come, and to watch her reaction. But at that moment Bernard arrived. He caught sight of Josée, and Fanny at once noticed the look of happiness on his face.

'Fanny, your husband has a business dinner and has sent me to fetch him a different tie because he won't have time to come home first. He told me he wanted his blue one with black stripes.'

They all three began to laugh. Fanny went out of the room to get the tie. Bernard took Josée's hands.

'Josée, I'm so happy to see you, but sad that it's

always for such a short time. Won't you have dinner with me?'

She glanced at him; he had a strange look, a mixture of bitterness and joy. His head was lowered, but she could see that his eyes were bright.

'He's like me,' she thought, 'we are the same sort, I ought to have loved him.'

'We'll have dinner together whenever you like,' she said.

For the past fortnight she had dined with Jacques at home, because, as he could not afford it, he did not want to go to a restaurant. He compromised with his pride by having dinner with Josée in her flat. After dinner he swotted for his exams while she read. At that moment it occurred to Josée, accustomed to amusing conversation and staying out late at night, that this kind of conjugal life with someone who hardly ever spoke was extraordinary. The bell rang and she loosened her hand from Bernard's.

'Someone is asking for Mademoiselle,' said the maid.

'Show him in,' said Fanny.

She was standing by the other door of the room. Bernard had already turned to face the hall.

'We might be on the stage,' thought Josée, beginning to giggle.

Jacques entered like a bull into the arena, his head lowered, pawing the carpet with his feet. He had a Belgian name that Josée was trying desperately to remember, but he anticipated her:

'I've come to fetch you,' he said.

His hands were in the pocket of his duffle-coat; he looked menacing.

'He's really unpresentable,' thought Josée, suppressing her desire to laugh, but she felt glad to see him and especially pleased when she noticed the look on Fanny's face. Bernard's expression gave nothing away; it seemed that he had suddenly become blind.

'You might say "how do you do",' said Josée almost tenderly.

Jacques smiled politely and shook hands with Fanny and Bernard. The setting sun over the rue de Tournon gave his hair a russet tinge.

'There is a phrase which describes that sort of man,' thought Josée: "I am the truth and the life."

'There is a word to describe that type of boy,' thought Fanny to herself: ' "hooligan", but where have I seen him before? Could it have been here?'

She remembered him vaguely and tried to be amiable.

'Do sit down. Why are we all standing? Will you have a drink? Or are you in a hurry?'

'I have plenty of time,' said Jacques. 'What about you?'

He spoke to Josée. She nodded.

'I must go,' said Bernard.

'I'll see you to the door,' said Fanny. 'You're forgetting the tie, Bernard.'

He was already at the front door, looking very pale. Fanny, who had been about to exchange signs of astonishment with him, did not do so. He left the house without a word. Fanny returned to the drawing-room. Jacques was sitting down, smiling at Josée.

'I bet you that was the fellow who telephoned,' he said.

*

Bernard walked along the street like someone possessed, almost talking aloud. At last he found a seat, sat down, and wrapped his arms round his body as if he were cold. 'Josée,' he thought, 'Josée and that brute!' He swayed in the throes of a real physical pain; an old woman sitting near looked at him with astonishment and a start of fear. He saw her, got up, and went on walking. He had to take the tie to Alain.

'This is too much,' he thought resolutely, 'it's intolerable. Bad novels, a ridiculous passion for a girl who isn't worth it! And though I don't love her, I'm jealous. It just can't go on, it is either too much or too little.' He decided to go away. 'I'll find some sort of cultural mission,' he thought sarcastically. 'That's all I'm capable of: articles on cultural subjects, journeys for the sake of culture, cultured conversation. Culture is for those who have nothing else.'

And what about Nicole? He would send her to her parents for a month, he would try to take himself in hand. But above all he must get away from Paris where Josée was. Where would she go with that boy, what would she do? He bumped into Alain on the stairs.

'At last you've brought my tie!' exclaimed Alain.

He was going to dine with Béatrice before the play. As she only appeared in the second act, they had until ten o'clock. Every moment of this time alone with her seemed precious to him. The pretext for the dinner was to talk about his young cousin Édouard. It was the first time Alain had found an excuse to see Béatrice except on the usual Mondays.

Wearing his new tie and, as usual, vaguely

worried about Bernard's pallor, Alain went to fetch Béatrice from her flat in a little side-street near the avenue Montaigne. He imagined; he was not sure what he imagined: Béatrice sitting opposite him in a restaurant which was luxurious but discreet, the sound of cars passing outside, and above all what he called the 'admirable mask' of Béatrice's face veiled by the pink light of a lampshade, leaning towards him. He thought of himself as he would appear in Béatrice's eyes, a sophisticated man with good taste and a tall figure (he knew this was important in Béatrice's eyes). They would talk of Édouard, first with indulgence, then with boredom, then they would pass to life in general, to the disillusion that life inevitably brings to beautiful women, and lastly they would talk of experience. He would take her hand across the table and could not imagine himself playing a more daring role. But he knew nothing of Béatrice's feelings. He was afraid of her, for he foresaw that she would be in good spirits and afflicted with that terrifying assurance which ambition imparts.

Nevertheless that evening Béatrice was acting a part which might well have harmonized with his plans. A few kind words from the producer of X's play, and the unexpected attention of an influential journalist, had led her, by one of those flights of fancy in which the imagination takes wing at the slightest encouragement, straight to the heights of success. And so, this evening she was the young actress with the world at her feet. So matching her dreams with reality by a miracle of compromise between time and sentimentality, which can only take place in the mind of a second-rate person, she was the triumphant young actress who preferred the conversation of a cultured man of letters to the frivolous pleasures of a night club; for success should not exclude originality. That is why she took Alain Maligrasse, although he had carefully planned a moderately extravagant evening, to a haunt frequented by intellectuals. So there was no pink lampshade between Alain and herself, but only the waitress's resentful hands, the noise of the people around them, and the whining of a guitar.

'My dear Alain,' said Béatrice in her low voice, 'what is it you want to talk to me about? I must say I was most intrigued by your telephone call.'

'It's about Édouard,' said Maligrasse nervously.

Time was passing so quickly! He crumbled his bread between his fingers. The first half-hour had been wasted in a taxi with Béatrice and the driver arguing as to the best way to find this infamous place, and then by Béatrice imploring the owner to find them a table. He could hardly breathe, and to make things worse he could see in a mirror the long, sagging lines of his face, wrinkled in some places and feebly childish in others. There are people in whom the signs of age are distributed haphazardly, so that they never look either young or old. He sighed.

'Are you thinking of Édouard?' Béatrice smiled.

'Yes,' he said, and her smile wrung his heart. 'What I'm going to say may sound silly to you, but Édouard is so young, and he's in love with you.'

'Heavens! How ridiculous this is,' thought Béatrice.

'Since he's been in Paris, he has borrowed more than a hundred thousand francs, half of it from Josée, so as to dress well and give you presents.'

'He simply showers me with flowers,' said Béatrice, smiling once more. Her smile was perfection, lazily indulgent, but Alain Maligrasse, who seldom went to a cinema or music hall, did not recognize it. It seemed to him so full of love for Édouard that he almost felt like leaving her and going home.

'It's rather a nuisance,' he said weakly.

'A nuisance that someone is in love with me?' asked Béatrice.

She bent her head and felt that by this gesture

she was disassociating herself from the subject of their conversation. But Alain's heart was beating fast.

'I understand only too well,' he said fervently. Béatrice almost laughed aloud.

'May I have some cheese?' she said. 'Talk to me about Édouard. I won't deny that he amuses me, but I don't wish him to borrow money on my account.'

For a moment she had thought of saying in a confidential voice: 'Well, let him ruin himself if he wants to. What are young men for?' But she was really too kind-hearted to feel this and besides it was hardly the right thing to say to someone so obviously concerned about a young relative. She leaned towards him as he had seen her do in his thoughts, the guitar became more plaintive, and the flicker of the candles was reflected in her eyes.

'What ought I to do, Alain? And honestly, what *can* I do?'

He drew a deep breath and began a long rambling explanation. Perhaps she could make Édouard understand that there was no hope for him?

'But there is,' thought Béatrice gleefully. She suddenly felt a great tenderness for Édouard, his fine auburn hair, his awkward gestures, his gay voice on the telephone. Fancy his borrowing money on her account! She forgot all about X's play and her part in it later that evening, and instead longed to see Édouard, to press him close, and feel him tremble with happiness. She had only seen him once in a bar since their first meeting, and he had been very shy, but seemed so dazzled by her appearance that she could not help being proud. For Édouard, her very existence was a priceless gift, and she had a vague feeling that all her relationships should be of the same kind.

'I'll do what I can,' she said. 'I promise for Fanny's sake. And you know I love her.'

'What a fool she is!' thought Maligrasse, but he stuck desperately to his plan, which was eventually to get close enough to Béatrice to hold her hand.

'How about going?' he said. 'Perhaps we could get a whisky somewhere before the second act. I'm not hungry.'

'We could go to Vat's,' thought Béatrice, 'but it's always so crowded – of course Alain is quite well known, but only among such a small circle, he looks like a lawyer's clerk in that tie. Dear Alain, he's so old-fashioned!' She stretched her hand over the table and took his.

'We'll go wherever you like,' she said, 'it makes me happy just to know that you exist!'

Alain wiped his mouth and almost in a whisper asked for the bill. Béatrice's hand, after patting his, slipped into a red glove, the same colour as her shoes. They had some whisky in a café opposite the theatre, and spoke of the war and of the post-war years – 'Young people today don't know what it is to dance to a jazz band in a cellar,' said Béatrice as they left. At ten o'clock they parted. For the past hour Alain had given up the struggle. He had listened to Béatrice as she talked of commonplace things and when he had the courage, he watched her face. Her high spirits made her a little flirtatious with him that evening, but he did not even notice it. When you have dreamed of something wonderful happening, a lesser pleasure, although it may be easier to achieve, hardly counts. Alain Maligrasse had read Stendhal with more pleasure than Balzac and now this cost him dear, for he had learned that you can despise what you love. Perhaps this saved him from trying to provoke a crisis, but on the other hand it might have been better for him in the end. At his age, passion can dispense with esteem more easily. But unlike Josée, he had not the happy certainty that the person he loved was his.

He returned home like a thief. If he had spent three hours with Béatrice at a hotel, he would have come back in triumph, with his conscience lightened by happiness. He had not been unfaithful to Fanny, so he crept home feeling guilty. Fanny was sitting up in bed wearing a blue bed-jacket. He undressed in the bathroom, talking vaguely of his business dinner. He felt exhausted.

When he kissed his wife she pulled him down to her until his face lay on her shoulder.

'Of course she's guessed everything,' he thought wearily. 'It is not this flabby shoulder that I need, but Béatrice's firm, rounded one; it is Béatrice's face, delirious with pleasure, that I want to see, not these intelligent eyes.'

'I am very unhappy,' he said aloud; then he loosened himself from Fanny's embrace and went to bed.

FOUR

BERNARD went away and Nicole wept. It was all just as he had foreseen. While he was packing his bags, it seemed to him that his life had followed an inevitable course from the beginning. The war had unsettled his childhood; there had been his affair with Béatrice, and a still longer attachment to literature. He had a good appearance and what could have been more normal than his marrying a rather insignificant young woman whom he was now making unhappy, although he did not know why! He was insensitive, and unknowingly exercised the small cruelties of a mediocre man, and had mediocre love affairs. But now he must play the part of the reassuring male. Seeing Nicole's tears he took her in his arms and said:

'Don't cry, dearest, you know it's better for me to go away. After all, what is a month? And your parents . . .'

'I don't want to go back to my parents, even for a month.'

This was Nicole's latest obsession: she wanted

to stay in their flat, and he knew that every night she would sleep with her face turned towards the door, waiting for him to return. He suddenly felt sorry for her and for himself.

'You'll be bored here all alone.'

'I'll go and see the Maligrasses and Josée has promised to take me out in her car.'

Josée! He let her go, picked up his shirts in a fury, and stuffed them into his bag. What did he care about Nicole or consoling her? Josée. When would he be free of that name and the jealousy it aroused in him? It was the only violent feeling he had ever experienced; and it had to be jealousy. He hated himself.

'You'll write to me, won't you?' said Nicole.

'Every day.'

He felt like saying: 'I could even write you thirty letters in advance: Dearest, all is well here. Italy is beautiful, one day we'll go there together. I have a lot of work to do, but I think of you and miss you. I'll write a longer letter tomorrow. Love and kisses.' That is what he would write to her for a whole month. How is it that some people inspire you and others don't? Ah, if it were Josée: 'Josée, if you only knew! I don't know how to make you understand what I feel, and I'm far away from you, from your face which, when I think of it, tears my

47

heart to pieces. Am I mistaken about you, Josée? Is there still time for us?' Yes, he was sure of it. He would know how to write to Josée from Italy, one night when he was feeling miserable and the words would flow heavy and strong from his pen and would come to life. After all, he knew how to write. But to Nicole . . . She was blonde and insipid, still whimpering a little as she leant against his back.

'I am sorry,' he said.

'It is I who should be sorry. I didn't know how . . . Oh, Bernard, I've tried so often . . .'

'What?' he said. He was apprehensive.

'I've tried to live up to your level, to help you, to be a companion, but I'm not clever enough, or amusing, or anything, and I know it quite well . . . Oh, Bernard!'

She was gasping. Bernard pressed her to him and asked her forgiveness again and again in a dead voice.

Soon he was on the road. Once again he was a man alone at the wheel, in a car lent him by his publisher. He found himself lighting a cigarette while driving with one hand, watching the play of headlights on the road, deciphering the signals of fear and friendship which one driver sends to another at night by means of the lights. He saw the vista of trees in full leaf looming up and then falling behind him. He was alone. He wanted to drive all night and experience fatigue. A kind of resigned happiness descended upon him. Perhaps all was lost, but what did it matter? He had always known that there was something else, something in himself, something exhilarating which he only felt when he was quite alone. Tomorrow there would be Josée who would again become the most important thing in his life, and he would commit a thousand acts of treachery, submit to a thousand defeats, but tonight after his fatigue and his sadness, he would reach that other thing which he would always find again, a quiet image of himself lulled by the foliage of the trees.

Nothing is more like one Italian town than another Italian town, particularly in the autumn. After spending six days visiting Milan and Genoa and doing some work in museums and libraries, Bernard decided to return to France. He wished to stay in a hotel in a provincial town. He chose Poitiers, which seemed to him the deadest place imaginable, and looked for the most ordinary hotel. He chose L'Écu de France. He chose this background deliberately, as he would have prepared a scene for a play. But he did not yet know what play he would perform or what part he would take in this setting, which according to the hour would recall Stendhal or Simenon. He did not know what failure or what shock of discovery awaited him. But he knew that he would be profoundly bored, probably in despair, and perhaps this boredom and despair would carry him through his impasse. After ten days' motoring he knew that it was neither his passion for Josée, nor his failure in literature, nor his disillusion in Nicole; but something lacking in his passion, in his failure and his disillusion, something which should have filled this early morning void and soothed his irritation with himself. Now he was laying down his arms and surrendering to the enemy. For three weeks he would have to bear with himself alone.

The first day he arranged his programme. The newspaper shop, the café where he took his apéritif, the small restaurant opposite with *specialités*, and the cinema at the corner. His hotel bedroom had a blue and grey wallpaper with a design of large faded flowers, an enamel washbasin, a dark brown jug; everything as it should be. Looking out of the window he could see an old advertisement hanging on the house opposite, 'The House of a Hundred Thousand Shirts', a closed window, which might possibly open, leaving a vague, romantic hope. His table was covered with a white cloth which was always slipping off. He had to remove it in order to write. The proprietress of the hotel was welcoming but reserved, the chambermaid old and loquacious.

There was a great deal of rain in Poitiers that year. Bernard settled in without irony or self-mockery. He treated himself as he would have done a stranger, bought a great many newspapers, and on the second day too many bottles of white wine and cassis. This gave him a dangerous feeling of elation which brought thoughts of Josée into his head.

'Waiter, how long does it take to get through to Paris on the telephone?' But he might not telephone after all.

He started his novel again. The first phrase was in a moralizing tone: 'Happiness is a sentiment that is more misunderstood than any other ...' This seemed true to Bernard. True, but futile. But there it was at the top of the page, *Chapter 1*. 'Happiness is a sentiment that is more misunderstood than any other. Jean-Jacques was a happy man but nobody had anything good to say of him.'

Bernard would have liked to begin differently: 'The straggling little village of Boissy appeared to the traveller as it lay there in the sunshine ...' However, he could not. He wanted to get at once to the essentials. But what were the essentials, and what did the essentials mean?

He wrote for an hour in the morning, went out to buy papers, to get shaved and have lunch. Then he worked for three hours in the afternoon, read a little Rousseau, and walked about until dinner. Afterwards there was the cinema, and once the local brothel, no worse than any other, where he realized that abstinence revives the taste for things.

The second week was much more difficult. His novel was bad. He re-read it dispassionately and realized how bad it was; worse than bad, not merely tedious and intensely tedious. He wrote in the same way as people cut their nails, attentively and absent-mindedly. He carefully observed his state of health, noticed the increased weakness of his liver, the irritable condition of his reflexes, both due to the stress of his life in Paris. One afternoon he looked at himself in the little mirror in his room and, closing his eyes, turned his face to the wall, and pressed his body with arms outstretched against the cold hard surface. He had sent a short, desperate note to Alain Maligrasse who had written advising him to look at others and turn away from himself. Stupid advice, as Bernard knew. No one has time to look deeply into himself and most people only gaze at others to see their own reflection.

Bernard, obscurely aware of his own limitations, had no intention of allowing himself to be rescued by a woman in Poitiers. In any case it would do him no good.

He was determined to go back to Paris with his manuscript, almost finished, under his arm. He would give it to his publisher, who would publish it. He would try to see Josée again and would ignore Nicole's reproachful looks.

It was all quite useless, but he drew a sort of peace from the conviction of his own uselessness. He knew in what pleasing terms he would speak of Poitiers and its distractions, what satisfaction he would derive from seeing the look of astonishment on people's faces when he recounted his escapade. Their glances would give him a sense of his originality. He would say, 'Above all, I worked'. He already knew exactly what form his pose would take, but he did not really care one way or another. At night he listened through the open window to the rain falling on Poitiers and followed with his eyes the golden headlights of the few passing cars as they illuminated the faded roses on the wall-paper. Lying quite still with his arms behind his head, he smoked his last cigarette of the day.

*

Édouard Maligrasse was no fool. He was a young man fated to be either happy or unhappy, but whom indifference would have destroyed. He was therefore delighted to find Béatrice and to love her, and it surprised her that merely to be allowed to love her made him happy. Most people consider love a catastrophe if it is not returned. This surprise gave him two weeks' advantage, which perhaps his good looks would not have done. Though Béatrice was not cold she had never much cared about physical love. Still, she thought it healthy and natural, and at one time even considered herself to be a woman dominated by her senses and passionate enough to have the right to be unfaithful to her husband. Since, in her circle, adultery had no great significance, she soon felt the need to call attention to it by a great scene of renunciation, which caused much suffering to her lover and annoyance to her husband, to whom she had confessed everything according to the rules of Act III. Since he was a sensible business man, her husband thought it absurd to confess she had a lover just at the moment she had decided to give him up. Much better to have said nothing, he said to himself while Béatrice, without make-up, went on reproaching herself in a monotonous voice.

Édouard Maligrasse, with a radiant face, waited for Béatrice at the stage door, he waited for her outside her hairdresser's and at the door of the concierge's office. He did not doubt that she would love him one day, and he waited patiently for her to give him what he believed to be the proof. Unfortunately Béatrice soon got accustomed to this platonic love affair, a situation which is very difficult to change, especially for a woman who is not intelligent. One evening Édouard took Béatrice home and asked if he could go up with her and have a drink. It must be said in his defence that he did not know the implication of this phrase. He was merely thirsty, having talked a great deal of his love, and had not a penny to go home with. The thought of a long, thirsty walk dismayed him.

'No, my dear Édouard,' said Béatrice tenderly, 'no, it is much better that you should go home.'

'But I'm terribly thirsty,' Édouard repeated; 'I don't need whisky, just a glass of water.'

He added shyly: 'Besides, I'm afraid all the cafés are shut at this time of night.'

They looked at each other. Édouard appeared particularly handsome in the lamplight, besides it was cold and Béatrice looked forward with some pleasure to refusing him in a scene played with grace and elegance. They went upstairs. Édouard re-lit the fire while Béatrice prepared a tray. They sat by the fire, Édouard took her hand and kissed it. Realizing the decisive moment had come, he trembled slightly. 'I am so happy that we are friends, Édouard,' she began dreamily. He kissed the palm of her hand.

'You see,' she continued, 'in the world of the theatre, which I love because I belong to it, the majority of people are . . . I will not say cynical, but without real youth. You are young, Édouard, and must remain so.'

She spoke with charming gravity. Édouard Maligrasse, in fact, felt extremely young at that moment; his cheeks were on fire, he pressed his lips to her wrist.

'I think you'd better go now,' she said suddenly, 'although you must know I trust you.'

If he had been a few years older, Édouard would have insisted. But he was not, and that saved him. He got up, excused himself, and walked towards the door. Béatrice was losing her chance to play the scene to the end; she knew she would be bored after he left, and she was no longer sleepy. There was only one thing to say:

'Édouard!'

He turned round.

'Come back.'

She held out her hands to him like a woman about to surrender. Édouard held them a long time, then, carried away by his youthful enthusiasm, seized Béatrice in his arms, searched for her mouth, and found it. He almost cried out with happiness, for he loved Béatrice. Late in the night he was still whispering words of love, his head on Béatrice's breast. She was fast asleep and knew nothing of the long-unfulfilled dreams which had inspired them.

FIVE

On waking beside Béatrice, Édouard experienced
one of those sensations of happiness which we
know at once justify our existence, but we also
know that they will be lost for ever when youth
has given way to the clearer vision of later years.
As he opened his eyes he saw Béatrice's shoulder
beside him, and memory, which dominates even
our dreams, came back to him. He was happy as
he stretched out a hand towards Béatrice's bare
back. But she considered sleep indispensable for her
good complexion. Her only genuine impulses were
hunger, thirst, and the desire for sleep. She moved
to the other side of the bed and Édouard found
himself alone.

He was filled with tender memories, but as she
turned away from him he became aware of the
elusiveness of love, and he was afraid. He would
have liked to turn her round to face him, to
put his head on her shoulder, and to thank her.
But he was powerless against that obstinate back
and her triumphant sleep. He caressed her long,

deceptively generous body through the sheets with a resigned gesture.

It was a symbolic awakening, but Édouard did not realize it. He did not know that his passion for Béatrice would henceforth be reduced to the contemplation of her back. We invent our own omens which seem bad when things are going against us. Édouard was not like Josée who, waking at the same moment, looked at her lover's smooth, hard back in the dawn, and smiled before going off to sleep again. But Josée was a great deal older than Édouard.

From then on life continued peacefully for Béatrice and Édouard. He fetched her from the theatre, and lunched with her whenever she wished. Actually Béatrice made a habit of lunching with women because she had read somewhere that this practice was very much the fashion in America; and also she thought she could learn something from studying her elders. So she often had lunch with old actresses who envied her growing success, and whose conversation would have given her an inferiority complex if she had not been made of stone.

Fame does not come with a sudden burst but grows gradually. It may occur from one day to another, and in Béatrice's case it took the form of a proposition from André Jolyet, a well-known theatre director and, amongst other things, an epicure. He offered her a good part in his next production in October, and in addition his villa in the South of France to work in.

Béatrice wanted to telephone to Bernard immediately; she considered him 'a clever young man' although he had often denied this. She was surprised to hear that Bernard was in Poitiers: 'What on earth can he be doing there?'

She telephoned to Nicole:

'I hear that Bernard is in Poitiers. What is he doing?'

'I don't know,' said Nicole, 'he's working.'

'How long has he been away?'

'For two months,' said Nicole, and burst into tears.

Béatrice was astonished. She imagined that Bernard must be madly in love with the wife of the Mayor of Poitiers; for how otherwise could he endure the provinces? Still, she had a kind heart and arranged to see Nicole, but afterwards received an invitation from André Jolyet, which she did not dare to refuse. She telephoned to Josée.

Josée was at home reading in her flat, where she never felt comfortable and where the telephone alternately irritated and soothed her. Béatrice explained the situation in exaggerated terms. Josée was mystified because the day before she had received a very fond letter from Bernard in which he analysed his love for her. She therefore found it difficult to believe he was interested in some mysterious woman in Poitiers. She said she would go and see Nicole, and went because she usually carried out her promises.

Nicole had grown fatter. Josée noticed it at once. Many women put on weight when they are unhappy, food seeming to reassure them in some vital way. Josée explained she had come instead of Béatrice, and Nicole, who was frightened of Béatrice and bitterly regretted her tears on the telephone, was relieved. Josée was thin, had mobile features, an air of adolescence, and the gestures of a thief. She seemed to Nicole, who had no idea of her circumstances, still more helpless than herself in the face of life's problems.

'Let's go into the country,' suggested Josée.

She drove well and fast in her big American car. Nicole huddled in the far corner. Josée's feelings were divided between boredom and a vague sentiment that she was fulfilling a duty. She thought of Bernard's letter:

'Josée, I love you and it is very painful for me. I

am trying to work here, but cannot do so. My life is a slow movement without music; I know you don't love me. Why should you? We are alike, but I am the incestuous one. I am writing you this because it is no longer important. I mean that it is no longer important whether I write to you or not. The only advantage of solitude is that you learn to accept yourself and renounce a certain form of vanity. Besides, there is that other young man and I do not like him . . .'

She remembered most of his letter. She had read it during breakfast while Jacques was reading *Le Figaro*, to which her father had given her a subscription. She had put the letter on the bedside table with an awful feeling of failure. Jacques had got up whistling and declared, as he did every morning, that there was nothing interesting in the paper. She could never understand the almost insane concentration with which he read newspapers. 'Perhaps he has murdered a rich woman,' she would think, half laughing, to herself. After his shower he came out of the bathroom wearing his duffle-coat and kissed her before going off to his lectures. She was surprised that she could still tolerate him.

'I know an inn where there is a wood fire,' she said to Nicole in order to break the silence.

She wanted to say: 'Your husband loves me, I don't love him; I will not take him away from you and he will get over it.' But it would have been betraying Bernard, and for Nicole any explanation would have been like an execution.

At lunch they talked of Béatrice. Then of the Maligrasses. Nicole was convinced they were in love with each other and absolutely faithful, and Josée did not undeceive her. She felt kindly towards Nicole, but weary. Nicole was three years older than she was: she could not do anything for her. Nothing at all. There is a form of feminine stupidity reserved for men. Josée gradually became more and more exasperated and contemptuous of Nicole, her hesitation with the menu, and her distraught look. While they were having coffee there was a long silence, suddenly broken by Nicole:

'Bernard and I are expecting a baby.'

'I thought so,' said Josée.

She knew that Nicole had had two miscarriages and been specially advised not to have children.

'I wanted to have one,' said Nicole.

She kept her head lowered, with an obstinate air. Josée looked at her in astonishment.

'Does Bernard know?'

'No.'

'Heavens!' thought Josée, 'she must be the normal, biblical kind of woman, who thinks it is sufficient to have a child to keep a man at her side, and puts him into an impossible situation. I shall never be like that; the poor girl must be terribly unhappy.'

'You must write and tell him,' said Josée firmly.

'I dare not,' said Nicole. 'First I want to be sure that nothing will happen.'

'I think you ought to tell him.'

If the same thing happened again and Bernard weren't there ... Josée was pale with fear. She could hardly imagine Bernard as a father, but Jacques on the other hand ... yes, Jacques would stand by her bed shyly and smile at his child. She must be getting quite delirious.

'Let's go home,' she said.

She drove slowly to Paris. When they reached the Champs-Élysées, Nicole caught her hand:

'Don't take me home just yet,' she said.

There was such a beseeching note in her voice that Josée suddenly realized what her life must be: the lonely waiting, the fear of death, and now her secret. She was overcome by pity. They went into a cinema. After ten minutes Nicole rose unsteadily from her seat and Josée followed her. The lavatories were horrible. She supported Nicole while she vomited, laid her hand on her damp forehead, and felt sick with horror and compassion.

When she got home she found Jacques who, when he had heard all about her day, expressed sympathy, and even called her 'poor old girl'. Then he suggested that they should go out, and for one evening gave up his medical studies.

SIX

FOR the next two days Josée tried to get Bernard
on the telephone to tell him to come home. He had
given orders that letters were to be addressed poste
restante. Josée tried to persuade Nicole to go to
Poitiers, but she obstinately refused; she was now
having constant pains which made Josée very
anxious. At last Josée decided to go herself to
Poitiers and bring Bernard back. She asked Jacques
to go with her, but he refused on account of his
lectures.

'But we could go there and back in a day,' Josée
insisted.

'That's why it is not worth my going.'

She felt inclined to hit him. He was always quite
decided about everything; life was so simple to
him; she would have given anything to see him at
a loss for once or trying to justify himself. He took
her firmly by the shoulders:

'You're a good driver and you like being alone.
Besides, it would be far better for you to see the
fellow by yourself. His relations with his wife have

nothing to do with me; only those concerning you are my affair.'

With these last words he looked straight at her.

'Oh, you know ... all that was a long time ago ...'

'I don't know anything,' he said. 'If I ever found out, I should go away.'

She looked at him in utter astonishment, and with a vague feeling that resembled hope.

'Would you be jealous?'

'It's not that. I just don't like half-shares.'

He suddenly pulled her towards him and kissed her cheek. Josée was so touched by the awkwardness of his movement, that she put her arms behind his head and pressed close to him. She kissed his neck and the shoulder of his rough jersey, smiling a little and repeating:

'You'd go away, you would actually go away?' in a pensive voice. But he did not move or say anything.

She felt as though she were in love with a bear she had met in a forest, a bear who perhaps loved her, but was unable to tell her so because he was a dumb animal.

'That's enough!' growled Jacques.

Early one morning she set off by herself in her car. She drove slowly through the wintry landscape. It was very cold and the pale sunshine gleamed down on the bare fields. Josée lowered the hood and put up the collar of the sweater she had borrowed from Jacques. She could feel the cold air on her face. The road was deserted. At eleven o'clock she stopped in a side road, pulled the gloves off her frozen hands, and lit a cigarette, the first since she had left home. She remained still for a moment, resting her head against the seat of the car and inhaling the smoke with her eyes closed. In spite of the cold she could feel the sunshine on her eyelids. It was absolutely quiet. When she opened her eyes she saw a crow alighting on the field near her.

She got out of the car and walked along the road between the fields. She walked with the same nervous steps as she did in Paris. She passed a farm and a few trees; the road continued straight as far as one could see. After a few minutes she looked round and saw her car by the roadside, black and faithful. She walked slowly back, feeling contented.

'There must be an answer to all this,' Josée said aloud, 'and even if there isn't . . .'

The crow flew off cawing loudly.

'I love these interludes,' she said, throwing her cigarette on to the ground and carefully crushing it with her foot.

She arrived at Poitiers at six o'clock and it took her a long time to find Bernard's address. The dark, pretentious hall of L'Écu de France looked sinister to her. She was taken up to Bernard's room through a long corridor covered with a beige cord carpet in which she caught her feet. Bernard was writing with his back to the door. He said, 'Come in' absent-mindedly. Surprised by the silence, he turned round. Suddenly Josée thought of his letter and of the interpretation he might put on her presence. She drew back. Bernard said, 'You've come!' and he held out his hands towards her. His expression changed completely at the sight of her and Josée had time to think: 'That is the face of a man when he is happy.' He held her against him, his head on her hair while she stood there petrified with no other thought than 'I must undeceive him. It is terrible, I must tell him.' But he was already talking, and every word became an obstacle to the truth.

'I did not hope ... I did not dare. It is too wonderful. How could I have lived here so long without you. Happiness is a strange thing ...'

'Bernard,' said Josée. 'Bernard.'

'You know, it's strange that one can never imagine how things are going to happen. I thought of our meeting as something violent, that I would

69

overwhelm you with questions, but it is as though I had found someone again whom I know very well. Someone I missed,' he added.

'Bernard, I must tell you . . .'

But she already knew that he would interrupt her and she would not speak.

'Don't say anything. It's so long since anything real has happened to me.'

'That is probably true,' thought Josée. 'He has a wife in danger who truly loves him, he is close to a real tragedy, but the only reality for him is this mistake, which I am allowing him to make. The happiness is true, but the love is false.'

She gave up all attempt to speak. It was easy to keep silent, because what she felt was neither pity nor irony, but an immense understanding. One day she would probably make a similar mistake, and, like him, she would imagine she was happy with someone who did not love her. He took her to have some white wine and cassis at the Café du Commerce. He talked a great deal, and well, about her and himself. It was a long time since Josée had really talked to anyone. She was overcome by fatigue and a feeling of compassion. Poitiers had closed round her: its grey and yellow street, the occasional passers-by dressed in black, the curious glances of customers in the café, and the bare branches of the plane trees, all these belonged to an unreal world that she had always known and had to rediscover.

That night Bernard lay asleep beside her. His long body was in her way and so was his possessive arm flung across her shoulders. For some time she watched the headlights of the cars, passing across the flowers on the wallpaper. It was very quiet. In two days she would tell Bernard he must go home. She would give him two days of her life, two happy days. Probably they would both have to pay dearly for them. She thought how Bernard must have lain awake through many long nights, as she was doing, contemplating those big, ugly flowers and watching the lights pass over them, and now it was her turn, even though she would be taking the path of lies.

SEVEN

ANDRÉ JOLYET had decided to make Béatrice
his mistress. He recognized that she had talent and
a ruthless determination to succeed; this combina-
tion interested him. He also appreciated Béatrice's
beauty, and the thought that they would make a
handsome couple satisfied his ever-present aesthetic
sensibility. At fifty years of age he was thin to the
point of looking dried up, with a disagreeable,
sarcastic expression and the sham gestures of a
young man, which had perhaps wrongfully earned
him the reputation of being a homosexual.
Aesthetic sensibility is often associated with curious
aberrations. André Jolyet was one of those men
who are considered eccentric, especially in artistic
circles, because they are too independent and
inclined to be offensive. He would have been
impossible had he not been so ready to make fun
of himself, as well as being very generous with
money.

It would have been easy for him to win Béatrice
by way of her ambition, but he knew too much

about that sort of thing to be amused by it. He made up his mind to gain an entry into her private world and play his part there, which he imagined to be something like that of Mosca – but a victorious Mosca – in *Chartreuse de Parme*. Of course he had not the stature of Mosca, but then neither was Béatrice a Sanseverina. Perhaps only young Édouard Maligrasse had something of Fabrice's charm. But what did Jolyet care? He liked commonplace themes and it was now rare for him to find a domestic drama in the cheerful mediocrity of his life.

Béatrice was caught between power and love, or rather, between the images of power and love. On one hand Jolyet, ironical, compromising, spectacular, and on the other, the gentle, good-looking, romantic Édouard. She was tremendously exhilarated. The agonies of having such a choice before her made life marvellous, although she had definitely decided on Jolyet for professional reasons. She was most generous in her favours towards Édouard and gave him many tokens of affection which he would certainly never have received if he had been the only man in her life, which shows that what is given with one hand is taken away with the other.

Jolyet had given Béatrice the principal part in his

new production, unconditionally. He had not in any way indicated his own intentions and had even complimented her on having such a charming young man as Édouard. But he had clearly let Béatrice understand that if she ever grew tired of Édouard, he would be happy to take her about. This was more than a mere expression of politeness, because he knew very well that women like Béatrice never leave one man except for another. At first Béatrice was enchanted with her role, but she soon became anxious and uncertain about Jolyet's feelings towards her. Édouard's love seemed insipid in comparison with Jolyet's suave indifference. She liked to conquer.

Jolyet took her one evening to dine at Bougival. It was a warm night and they walked beside the river. She had told Édouard that she was going to dinner with her mother, a strict Protestant, who disapproved of her daughter's way of life. The need for this lie, which had cost her nothing to tell, had particularly annoyed her. 'I don't have to account for my actions to anyone,' she thought angrily while she was lying to Édouard. In any case Édouard asked nothing more than that she should allow him to be happy, and he was merely disappointed not to be having dinner with her. She imagined that he was jealous and suspicious. It was beyond her understanding that he loved her with the utter confidence of a true lover.

Jolyet held Béatrice's arm as they walked, giving only part of his attention to her exclamations of joy at the sight of some barges. Whereas with Édouard she liked to act the disillusioned *femme fatale*, with Jolyet she played the unrestrained eager child.

'How lovely it is here!' she exclaimed. 'No one has ever really described the Seine and its barges, except perhaps Verlaine . . .'

'Perhaps . . .'

Jolyet was delighted with her. He watched Béatrice embark on one of her long poetic effusions. 'Perhaps after all the reason I pursue her is because she amuses me,' he thought; and the idea gave him pleasure.

'When I was young . . .' (Béatrice waited for a laugh, which came.) 'When I was very small,' she went on, 'I used to walk like this beside the water, and I said to myself life was full of beautiful things, and I was full of enthusiasm. Would you believe it, I haven't changed?'

'I believe you,' said Jolyet, more and more pleased.

'And yet nowadays, who cares about barges, or gets excited about them? Neither in books, nor in the cinema or the theatre . . .'

Jolyet nodded without replying.

'I remember that when I was ten years old,' began Béatrice in a dreamy voice . . . She interrupted herself. 'But how can my childhood interest you?'

The suddenness of her attack left Jolyet without an answer. He had a moment of panic.

'I would rather you talked to me of *your* childhood,' said Béatrice. 'I know so little about you. You are a sort of enigma to those who surround you.'

Jolyet searched his mind desperately for some childhood memory, but could find nothing.

'I had no childhood,' he said impressively.

'You do say dreadful things!' said Béatrice, squeezing his arm.

No more was heard of Jolyet's childhood, but Béatrice's was enriched by numerous anecdotes to show off her ingenuousness, her waywardness, and her charm. She grew more and more sentimental. Her hand and Jolyet's finished up together in his pocket.

'How cool your hand is,' he said contentedly.

She did not answer, but leaned against him. Jolyet knew she was his and asked himself for a moment if he really desired her, since attainment interested him so little? He took her back to Paris.

In the car she put her head on his shoulder and sat very close to him. 'That's that!' thought Jolyet with a sense of fatigue, and he took her to her flat because it was there he wished to spend their first night. Like many people who are weary, he preferred fresh surroundings for his amorous adventures. But by the time they reached Béatrice door, her silence and immobility showed that she was fast asleep. He gently woke her, kissed her hand, and put her into the lift before she had come to life.

Édouard was asleep in front of the dying fire, his open shirt collar showing his slender, brown neck, like a girl's. Béatrice's eyes filled with tears. She was distressed because she still did not know whether she could depend upon Jolyet's devotion and also because Édouard was so handsome, though she was completely indifferent to this except when they were dining out. She woke Édouard up. He told her sleepily that he loved her. This was no consolation and when he wanted to come to her room, she pretended she had a migraine.

Meanwhile Jolyet walked home in good spirits, followed a woman for a while, then went into a bar, where he found Alain Maligrasse, drunk for the first time in the twenty years he had known him.

*

After his evening with Béatrice, Alain Maligrasse decided not to see her again. It was unbearable to love anyone so different from himself, so unresponsive. Only work could save him. Fortunately, Bernard's absence gave him a great deal more to do than usual. So he tried, helped by Fanny's discreet support, to forget Béatrice. Of course he did not succeed, though he avoided seeing her. He found himself inducing Édouard to come to his house as often as possible, and suffered tortures by observing the signs of happiness in him. He even persuaded himself that a cut from a razor on Édouard's neck was the mark of Béatrice's teeth in spite of Bernard's scornful laugh, for he still believed her to be passionate and his interpretation of the shadows under Édouard's eyes caused him acute suffering. Alain spent long hours in his office going through new manuscripts, writing copious notes, and filling in cards for his files. With a ruler he would begin to underline the title on the card in green ink, then his hand would lose control and the line slur as his heart began beating at the sudden recollection of something Béatrice had said during that memorable dinner. He would throw the card into the waste-paper basket and start all over again. In the street he bumped into passers-by; he no longer greeted his friends, and gradually became the absent-minded charming intellectual that everyone expected him to be.

Whenever Alain opened a newspaper he turned at once to the theatre page hoping to find some mention of Béatrice, which he often did; then he cast his eye down the list of theatre advertisements, until he saw her name in small letters under the title of the play at the Ambigu Theatre. He at once looked up guiltily and then switched quickly to other parts of the paper without taking them in. The day before he met Jolyet in the bar he had read a notice saying 'No Tuesday Performance', and his heart missed a beat. He knew that he could always see Béatrice for ten minutes every evening on the stage, and had resisted the temptation, but the thought that for once she would not be there appalled him. He would not have gone that evening in any case, but this did not occur to him. Béatrice, so beautiful and impetuous! He hid his eyes with his hand. He could not bear it another moment. When he got home he found Édouard there; he told him that Béatrice was dining with her mother. But this was no consolation. The harm was done. Alain realized how deeply he cared. He pretended to have a dinner in town, hung about miserably in the Café de Flore where he met some friends, who, seeing how pale he looked, insisted on his drinking two whiskies, the worst possible thing for his liver. He continued to drink, and at midnight found himself beside Jolyet in this sordid little bar near the Madeleine.

Alain was in a bad way. Alcohol always disagreed with him. His eyelids were swollen and his pale, sensitive face twitched noticeably. Jolyet was surprised but shook hands effusively. He liked Alain very much and had never expected to find him drunk and alone in such a place. Jolyet was torn between curiosity, sadism, and friendship – the kind of conflicting sentiments that could be sure of rousing his interest. Quite naturally they began to talk of Béatrice.

'I believe you've given her a part in your next play,' said Alain who felt rather gay and exhausted. The bar was swaying round him. He had reached a stage of intoxication where people are obsessed by themselves, and have no need of others.

'I've just had dinner with Béatrice,' said Jolyet.

'So she is a liar,' thought Maligrasse, remembering what Édouard had told him.

However he was rather pleased because the lie made him realize that she did not love Édouard. But if Béatrice was a liar, she would be more inaccessible to him than ever, unless she had some delicacy of feeling. All the same, his first reaction was one of relief.

'She's a nice girl,' he said, 'charming.'

'She is beautiful,' said Jolyet with a short laugh.

'Beautiful and impetuous,' said Alain, repeating his definition, and he said it in such a way that Jolyet turned to look at him. They eyed each other in silence, both thinking how little they knew one another in spite of their apparent familiarity.

'I have a weakness for her,' said Alain in a tone he tried to keep as light as possible.

'That is very natural,' said Jolyet.

Although he felt inclined to laugh, he longed to console Alain. His first thought had been: 'That should be easily arranged!' Then he realized this was not true. Béatrice would be more likely to give herself to a rich old roué than to Alain. In love, as in business, only the rich can live on credit, and Alain was obviously very poor. Jolyet ordered two more whiskies. He knew that they had a long night before them, and was delighted. More than anything he enjoyed observing the changing expression on a face, feeling a glass between his fingers, low-voiced confidences, nights lasting until dawn, and finally a pleasant sensation of fatigue.

'What can I do at my age?' said Alain.

Jolyet shuddered. 'Everything!' he replied in a firm voice. They were the same age.

'She's not meant for me,' said Alain.

'No one is ever "meant" for anyone,' hazarded Jolyet.

'Yes, Fanny was meant for me. That is the worst part. My obsession . . . I feel ridiculous and old. But it's the only thing that seems alive to me. All the rest . . .'

'Yes, I know; all the rest is literature,' said Jolyet with a short laugh. 'The trouble is that Béatrice is not intelligent but she's ambitious, and that is greatly in her favour at the present time, when people are so negative.'

'I could give her something that she probably does not know, confidence, consideration, a certain refinement, in fact . . . and then . . .'

He stopped when he saw Jolyet's look, and made a vague gesture which upset some of his whisky on to the floor. He apologized profusely to the proprietress. Jolyet felt acute pity for him.

'Try to explain everything to her, old man; even if she refuses, you will have broken the ice, and you'll know where you are.'

'Tell her now? When she's in love with my young cousin? It would mean sacrificing my only chance, if I have one.'

'You are mistaken. For certain people there is a right and a wrong time, though in Béatrice's case time has nothing to do with it.'

Maligrasse passed his hand over his hair, but there was so little of it that the gesture was merely pathetic. Jolyet vaguely searched for some means of giving Béatrice to his dear old friend, after he had finished with her himself of course. He could think of no way, and ordered two more drinks. Meanwhile, Maligrasse continued talking about love. A girl was listening and nodded agreement. Jolyet, who knew her well, asked her to look after Alain, and left. The pale, damp dawn was breaking over the Champs-Élysées, the early morning perfume of Paris recalled the country and made him stop a moment and breathe deeply before lighting a cigarette. He smiled, murmured 'Delightful evening', then walked briskly homewards with the step of a young man.

EIGHT

'I'LL telephone tomorrow,' said Bernard, putting his head through the car door. He probably felt a vague relief at their separation, as often happens after the most intense passions. At last there is time to be happy. Josée smiled at him. She was pleased to be back in the Paris night, the noise of the traffic, and her own life.

'Hurry up!' she said.

She saw him enter his doorway and drove off. She had told him the day before of the risk Nicole was running and that he must go home. She expected him to be very much shocked, but his only reaction had been to say:

'Is that why you came?'

She had replied 'no' and no longer knew to what extent her answer had been dictated by cowardice. Perhaps she wished, as much as he did, to protect those three grey days in Poitiers and their strange sweetness: leisurely walks in the frozen countryside, long talks, tender embraces at night, all based upon a misunderstanding which made everything unreal and strangely honest.

She got back to her flat at about eight o'clock and hesitated before inquiring from the maid about Jacques. She learned that he had gone away two days after her departure, leaving a pair of shoes behind. Josée telephoned to his old address, but he had moved; they did not know where he was. The light fell on the carpet in her large sitting-room; distraught with fatigue, she looked at herself in the mirror. She was twenty-five years old, had three wrinkles and a longing for Jacques. She had vaguely hoped to find him there in his duffle-coat and be able to explain to him how unimportant her absence had been. She telephoned to Fanny who invited her to dinner.

Fanny had grown very thin; Alain seemed far away. Fanny tried desperately to make polite conversation which was almost unbearable to Josée. As soon as they had finished coffee, Alain got up and said he was going to bed. For a few moments Fanny resisted Josée's questioning look and went over to arrange something on the mantel-piece. She was very small.

'Alain had too much to drink last night, you must excuse him.'

'Really?'

Josée laughed. Surely that was most unlike him!

'Don't laugh!' said Fanny quickly.

Fanny explained that Alain's infatuation for Béatrice was ruining both their lives. Josée tried in vain to convince her that it couldn't last long: 'Béatrice is an impossible person. He'll soon give her up. She's charming, but she has no feeling whatever. One-sided love cannot last. Has she . . .?' She did not dare to ask 'Has she yielded to him?' How could anyone 'yield' to a man as polite as Alain?

'No, of course not,' said Fanny angrily. 'I was wrong to have mentioned it. Forgive me, it's just that I feel so lonely.'

Josée left her at midnight. She had been afraid all the time that Alain would return, attracted by the sound of their voices. The thought of unhappiness and hopeless passion frightened her and she went away feeling bewildered by life's complexity.

At all costs she must find Jacques, even if he was violent and rejected her. She drove to the Latin Quarter.

It was a dark rainy night in Paris. Exhausted as she was, Josée dreaded this absurd, almost hopeless, hunt for Jacques. He must be somewhere in one of the cafés on the boulevard Saint-Michel, or at a friend's flat, or perhaps with a woman. This district, and the cellar where they all used to dance, seemed unfamiliar now that it had been given over to tourists. Having thought of him as a typical rough student, which was what his appearance and behaviour seemed to indicate, she now realized that Jacques' world was quite unknown to her. Although she tried desperately to remember some name or address he might have mentioned, none occurred to her. The whistles and rude remarks of the men in the cafés she entered, during her search, struck her like so many blows. It was a long time since she had lived through such moments of anguish, and the probable uselessness of her search, combined with the thought of Jacques' angry face, increased her despair.

In the tenth café she saw him. He had his back to the door and was playing mechanical billiards. There was no mistaking him as he bent over the table, his straight neck covered with coarse, fair hair. For a moment it seemed to her that his hair was too long, like Bernard's, and she wondered whether this was a peculiarity of men who had been deserted for another. Her heart missed a beat, and for several minutes she stood there unable to move.

'Do you want something?'

The proprietor of the café came to the rescue.

Josée stepped nearer, her coat was far too elegant for such a place, and she instinctively turned up her collar. She called: 'Jacques!' He did not turn round immediately, but she saw a red flush spreading from his neck to the side of his cheek.

'Do you want to speak to me?' he asked her at last.

They sat down without his looking at her. He asked in a hoarse voice what she wanted to drink, then lowered his eyes and deliberately stared at his short square hands.

'You must try to understand,' said Josée, beginning her story in a listless voice because she realized that Poitiers, Bernard, and all she had felt there were unreal and useless. Once more she was with Jacques, this solid block of a man who was to decide her fate, and whom words hardly touched.

'I don't like being made to look a fool,' said Jacques. She waited for him to continue.

'It is not that at all . . .' began Josée.

He raised his eyes. He looked white with fury.

'But it is. When you live with one man, you don't go off and spend three days with another, that's all. Or, if so, you tell him beforehand.'

'I've tried to explain . . .'

'I don't care a damn for your explanation. I'm not a child. I am a man. I even left my own room

to come and live with you,' he added still more
furiously: 'And there aren't many girls for whom
I would have done that. How did you find me?'

'For the past hour I've been searching every
café,' said Josée.

She closed her eyes with utter exhaustion, and
seemed to feel their weight on her cheeks. There
was a moment of silence, then he asked her in a
stifled voice:

'Why?'

She looked at him without understanding.

'Why have you been searching for me for an
hour?'

She had closed her eyes again and leant her head
back. An artery was beating in her throat. She
heard herself reply:

'I needed you,' and her eyes filled with tears.

That night he went home with her: when he
took her in his arms she knew once more that he
was the only lover she wanted. She kissed his hand
and went to sleep with her lips against his palm.
He remained awake for some time, then carefully
covered her shoulders with the sheet before
turning away.

NINE

On returning home Bernard found two hospital nurses at the door, one arriving and the other leaving. He felt sure there had been a disaster, and he knew he was incapable of dealing with it. He was frozen. The nurses told him that Nicole had had a miscarriage two days previously, and though she was now out of danger Dr Marin decided she must have a nurse in constant attendance. They stared at him, judged him, and no doubt thought he owed them an explanation. Without a word he pushed past them and went straight into Nicole's bedroom.

Her head was turned towards him in the dim light cast by a low porcelain lamp, a gift from her mother which Bernard had never dared to say he thought hideous. She was very pale and her face did not change when she saw him. She had the expression of a resigned animal, obtuse and dignified.

Bernard sat down on the bed and took her hand. She looked at him calmly, suddenly her eyes filled with tears. He carefully put his arms round her and she let her head sink on to his shoulder. 'What can I say or do?' thought Bernard. 'What a swine I am.' He stroked her head and, getting his fingers entangled in her long hair, tried mechanically to disentangle them. She was still feverish. 'I must say something,' thought Bernard, 'I must talk to her.'

'Bernard,' she said, 'our child . . .'

She began to cry. He could feel her shoulders shaking as he held her. 'There, there,' he said trying to soothe her. And suddenly he realized that this was his wife, his property, she belonged to him, she thought only of him, and had nearly died. She was his only possession, and he had nearly lost her. He was so moved by these thoughts that he turned his head away. We cry when we are born, and what follows can only be an attenuation of this cry. The strange feeling that rose to his throat left him weakly clinging to the shoulders of this woman whom he no longer loved. His life had been nothing more than one long retreat from reality, mere playacting. For a moment he forgot Josée, and gave himself up entirely to his despair.

Later he comforted Nicole as best he could. He was affectionate, spoke of their future, of his book, with which he said he was satisfied, and of the children they would soon have. She told him tearfully that she had wanted to call this one Christophe. He approved and suggested Anne; she laughed because everyone knows that men prefer daughters. All the same he searched for some means of telephoning to Josée that evening. He soon found a pretext: he had run out of cigarettes.

The cashier welcomed him with a gay 'Back at last!' and he drank a cognac at the zinc counter before telephoning. He intended to tell Josée that he needed her, which was true, and that nothing would be changed. When he spoke to her of their love she invariably replied, 'Love does not last: in a month or two you'll have forgotten all about me.' Josée was the only person he knew who was conscious of time. Others, following some inherent instinct, believed that love was eternal and would put an end to loneliness, and he was like them.

There was no answer from Josée's flat. He remembered that other night when he had telephoned, and her dreadful young man had answered. He smiled with pleasure at the thought that Josée was probably fast asleep, her hand open, palm upwards, the only indication she ever gave that she needed anyone.

*

Édouard Maligrasse was pouring out tisane which Béatrice had been drinking lately for health reasons. He gave her a cup and then passed one to Jolyet who laughingly said it tasted horrible. The two men then had some whisky. Béatrice pretended they were drunkards and Édouard, perfectly happy, leaned back in his armchair. They had just fetched Béatrice from the theatre, and she had asked Jolyet to come up to her flat for a drink. It was raining, but they were warm and comfortable there and Jolyet was entertaining.

Béatrice was furious. It irritated her that Édouard should be serving tisane and playing the part of the master of the house. Besides, it was compromising. She forgot that Jolyet knew about their liaison. No one is more particular about the conventions than a woman who is tired of her lover. Béatrice even forgot that she had taught Édouard to perform these menial tasks.

She began to discuss the play with Jolyet, obstinately refusing to allow Édouard to join in the conversation, in spite of Jolyet's attempts to include him. At last Jolyet turned to Édouard and asked:

'How's the insurance business?'

'Very good,' said Édouard.

He blushed. He owed a hundred thousand francs to his boss, which represented two months' salary, and fifty thousand francs to Josée, but tried not to think of it, although he had worried about it all day.

'That would be just the job for me,' said Jolyet light-heartedly. 'It's a quiet life and you don't have the worry of trying to raise the money to produce plays.'

'I can't imagine you doing that sort of work,' said Béatrice, 'it's almost like going from door to door . . .' She gave an insulting little laugh at Édouard's expense.

He did not move, but looked at her in amazement. Jolyet came to the rescue:

'On the contrary, I would be very good at selling insurance. All my powers of persuasion would be brought to bear: "Madame, you look very ill, you might die at any moment, you should insure yourself so that your husband has a little nest egg when he remarries"'

He roared with laughter, but Édouard feebly protested:

'In any case, that is not part of my work, I have an office, but it's very boring,' he added, afraid of having made himself seem too important, 'actually, my job is statistics . . .'

'Will you have some more whisky, André?' interrupted Béatrice.

There was a moment of silence; Jolyet made a desperate effort:

'No, thank you. I once saw a very good film called *Death Insurance*. Did you see it?'

The question was addressed to Édouard, but Béatrice could not control herself. She wanted Édouard out of the way and it looked as though he intended to stay, which was natural enough since he had lived with Béatrice for the past three months. He would remain there and sleep in her bed and the whole thing bored her to death. She tried to pay him out.

'You know Édouard comes from the provinces.'

'I saw the film in Caen,' said Édouard.

'What a marvellous place Caen must be!' scoffed Béatrice.

Édouard got up feeling dizzy. He seemed so hurt that Jolyet promised himself to make Béatrice suffer for this one day.

Once he was up, Édouard hesitated. He could not believe that Béatrice no longer cared for him, or even that he got on her nerves. He had never envisaged such a possibility. It would have ruined his present life. He said politely:

'Am I in the way?'

'Not at all,' said Béatrice furiously.

He sat down again, for he hoped that in the warmth of their bed that night, he would be able to question her. The best answer would be the sight of her beautiful, tragic face lying next to his in the half-light. He loved Béatrice physically, in spite of her coldness, in fact this added to her attraction for him. He would lie for hours propped on one elbow watching her as she lay asleep.

That night she was more distant than ever towards him. Béatrice never felt remorse, and this was part of her charm. He slept very badly and began to realize the extent of his misfortune.

As she was not certain of Jolyet's feelings towards her, Béatrice hesitated to get rid of Édouard. No one had ever loved her so desperately and so unreservedly, and she knew it. All the same, she began to see him less frequently and he often found himself alone in Paris.

Paris was reduced for him to two circuits: one lay between his office and the theatre, and the other from the theatre to Béatrice's flat. Everyone is familiar with these infinitely small circumferences which love creates in the heart of a great city. All of a sudden Édouard felt himself lost. He continued to follow the same paths, but as Béatrice's dressing-room was forbidden him, he took a seat at the theatre every evening. He paid little attention to the play but waited in suspense for Béatrice's entrance. She was taking the part of a lady's maid, and appeared in the second act, saying to a young man who had come to fetch her mistress before the appointed hour:

'You will learn, sir. For a woman, the right time is often the right time. After the right time is also sometimes the right time, but before the right time is never the right time.'

For some reason this insignificant sentence tore Édouard's heart to shreds. He waited for it after the three cues which he knew by heart, and he closed his eyes while Béatrice was speaking.

He was reminded of the happy time when Béatrice did not have so many business engagements, attacks of migraine, and luncheons with her mother. He dared not say 'When Béatrice loved me,' for however much he deluded himself in other ways he had always realized that he was the lover and she the beloved. It gave him a bitter satisfaction to think that she could never say she no longer loved him.

In spite of drastic economies on his midday meal, he was soon unable to afford even a folding seat at the theatre. His meetings with Béatrice became more and more rare. He dared not say anything. He was afraid, and as he did not know how to act a part, their interviews consisted of his dumb and passionate questions which disturbed Béatrice's morale. She was busy learning her part in Jolyet's next production and hardly had time to notice Édouard's face, or, for that matter, Jolyet's. At last she had a part, a real part, and the mirror in her room was now her greatest friend. It no longer reflected a tall young man with chestnut hair, but the passionate heroine of a nineteenth-century drama. Édouard took to walking round Paris, covering ten or fifteen kilometres a day, to distract himself from his unhappiness and his longing for Béatrice. His emaciated face with its haunted look attracted women as he passed by and many would have been willing to console him had he even noticed them. He was trying to understand what had happened, what he had done to make him unworthy of Béatrice. He could not know that, on the contrary, he was far too good for her and that was unpardonable.

One evening, when he was particularly distressed and had not eaten for two days, he went to the Maligrasses' flat. He was surprised to find Alain lying on the divan reading a theatrical magazine instead of his usual *Nouvelle Revue Française*. They exchanged glances, each equally surprised to find the other looking so distraught, and little suspecting that it was for the same reason. Fanny came into the room, kissed Édouard, and expressed her astonishment that he looked so ill. She herself, on the other hand, looked rejuvenated and cheerful. She had made up her mind to take no notice of Alain's behaviour, to pay frequent visits to a beauty parlour, and to make sure that he would find the house attractive. She knew very well that this was the usual recipe in women's magazines, but as intelligence seemed to have nothing to do with the situation she did not hesitate. Her first anger having passed, she only desired Alain's happiness, or at least his peace of mind.

'My dear Édouard, you seem tired. Is it overwork? You must take care of yourself.'

'I'm awfully hungry,' Édouard confessed.

Fanny laughed.

'Come with me to the kitchen, there's some ham and cheese left over.'

They were going out of the room when Alain's voice stopped them; it sounded quite non-committal.

'Édouard, have you seen the photograph of Béatrice in this number of *Opéra*?'

Édouard leapt to the sofa to look over Alain's

shoulder. It was a photograph of Béatrice in evening dress. *Young Béatrice B. rehearses the principal role in Jolyet's new play at the Athena.* Fanny looked for a second at her husband's back, at Édouard's back, close together, strained towards the paper, then she turned on her heel. She glanced at herself in the small mirror in the kitchen and said aloud: 'All this gets on my nerves.'

'I'm going out,' said Alain.

'Are you coming home tonight?' asked Fanny in a low voice.

'I don't know.'

He did not look at her, he never looked at her now. He spent his nights drinking with the girl from the bar at the Madeleine, ending up in her room, usually without touching her. She told him stories about her clients to which he listened attentively. She had a room near the St Lazare Station, a street lamp shone through the shutters marking the ceiling with parallel bars. When Alain had drunk a great deal he fell asleep at once. He had no idea that Jolyet paid the girl to look after him, and he attributed her kindness to affection which, in fact, she soon began to feel for this gentle, well-bred man. Fanny's good humour reassured him, but usually he tried not to think of her.

Fanny watched indulgently while Édouard devoured his food.

'How long is it since you had a meal?' she asked him. He raised his eyes to hers and their warmth and kindness overwhelmed him with gratitude. He softened a little. He had been too much alone, too unhappy and Fanny was too kind. He hastily drank a glass of beer to loosen the grip which held his throat.

'Two days.'

'No money?'

He nodded. Fanny was indignant.

'You're mad, Édouard. Surely you know this house is always open to you. Come whenever you like, without waiting till your last gasp. It's ridiculous.'

'I am ridiculous, and I know it!' exclaimed Édouard.

The beer had gone to his head. For the first time he envisaged getting over his passion. There were other things in life: friendship, affection, and above all the sympathy of someone like Fanny, that marvellous woman whom his cousin had been wise and fortunate enough to marry. They went into the drawing-room. Fanny picked up her knitting to which she had taken for the past month. Knitting is a great resource for unhappy wives.

Édouard sat at her feet. They lit a fire and both of them felt better.

'Tell me what is wrong,' said Fanny. She was sure he would talk of Béatrice and she began to feel a certain curiosity about her. Fanny had always thought her beautiful, vivacious, and rather stupid. Perhaps Édouard would explain the secret of her charm. She still thought that it was not Béatrice herself whom Alain was pursuing, but an idea.

'You know that we ... that is Béatrice and I ...'

Édouard was getting confused. Her understanding smile made him blush and at the same time a desperate feeling of loss swept over him. Everyone had taken for granted that he was happy as Béatrice's lover. Now it was all over. In a broken voice he began his story, but the more he tried to explain the cause of his misery, the more wretched he became, and he finished up sobbing with his head on Fanny's knee. She stroked his hair saying 'Poor darling' over and over again in a comforting voice. She was disappointed when he raised his head, for she liked the soft feel of his hair.

'Forgive me,' said Édouard, embarrassed. 'I've been alone so long.'

'I know what it is like,' said Fanny without thinking.

'Alain . . .?' began Édouard.

He stopped, suddenly remembering Alain's strange behaviour earlier that evening and his disappearance. Fanny believed he knew all about it, and spoke openly of her husband's folly. The look of stupefaction on his face made her realize that Édouard knew nothing. Alain would have found his astonishment most offensive, for the thought that his cousin could love and desire Béatrice horrified Édouard. He became aware of Fanny's sadness and took her hand. By now he was sitting on the sofa with her, worn out with misery, and he suddenly crumpled up sideways with his head on her shoulder. She put down her knitting. He fell into a light sleep. Fanny switched off the light so that he should sleep better. She did not move and hardly dared to breathe. Édouard's breath fanned her neck: she found his nearness perturbing but tried not to think about it.

After an hour Édouard woke up. He found himself in the dark, resting on a woman's shoulder. His first gesture was instinctive. Fanny held him very close. Others followed. At dawn he opened his eyes in a strange bed and saw a thin hand covered with rings lying on the sheet beside him.

He averted his eyes, got up, and fled. Fanny pretended to be asleep.

*

Josée telephoned to Bernard the next day. She said she must talk to him. He realized immediately what it meant – he had always understood. He loved Josée and needed her, but she did not love him. Therein lay the core of his weakness and suffering, and it would take him a long time to conquer it. The three days in Poitiers would be his only gift from fate that year, the only occasion when happiness might have made a man of him, for misfortune teaches nothing and resignation is ugly.

It was pouring with rain and everyone said that it was not like spring. Bernard went to his last meeting with Josée on foot and found her waiting for him. Then everything happened as he had expected, like a scene always known to him.

They sat on a bench in the rain, which never ceased. They were dead tired. She told him she did not love him and he replied that it did not matter, and the poverty of their words brought tears to their eyes. It was one of those benches in the Tuileries Gardens overlooking the Place de la Concorde with its endless traffic. The lights of the city glowed mercilessly like memories of childhood. They held hands and his face, wet with tears, touched Josée's, wet with rain. They exchanged passionate lovers' kisses; they were both ill-fated people, but they did not care. They were fond of each other. The damp cigarette that Bernard tried unsuccessfully to light was symbolic of their lives, for they would never know real happiness and were aware of it, but they also felt that it was not at all important.

*

A week after his evening with Fanny, Édouard received a summons from his tailor. He had spent his last money on flowers for her, and, although he did not know it, she had been almost moved to tears when they arrived. The only person to whom Édouard could turn was Josée, although he had borrowed from her before. However, he went to see her one Saturday morning. She was not at home; instead he found Jacques deep in his medical books. Jacques told him that Josée would be in for lunch and went back to his room to work.

Édouard paced up and down the drawing-room, in despair at having to wait. His courage evaporated, and he began to think up some excuse for his visit. Jacques soon returned, gave him a vague glance, then sat down and offered him a cigarette. The silence grew unbearable.

'You don't look very happy,' he remarked.

Édouard nodded his head, and Jacques looked at him with sympathy.

'It's not my business, but I've seldom seen anyone appear so worried.'

He almost gave a whistle of admiration. Édouard smiled at him. He found himself liking Jacques, who was very different from the young men he had met in the world of the theatre, and different also from Jolyet. Édouard began to feel himself a man again.

'Women!' he said briefly.

'Poor chap!' said Jacques.

There was a long silence filled with memories, then Jacques coughed:

'Is it Josée?'

Édouard shook his head. He felt he wanted to impress Jacques.

'No, an actress.'

'I don't know any, but they can't be easy to deal with.'

'They are not!' said Édouard.

'I'll go and find something to drink,' said Jacques.

He got up, gave Édouard a rough but friendly

slap on the shoulder as he passed, and returned with a bottle of Bordeaux. By the time José arrived they both looked very contented, were on terms of familiarity and talking lightly about women.

'Good morning, Édouard, you don't look at all well.'

She liked him and found his helplessness rather touching.

'How is Béatrice?'

Jacques made a sign to her which Édouard intercepted; they all looked at one another, and Josée burst out laughing.

'I suppose things aren't going well. Why don't you have lunch with us?'

They spent the afternoon together in the woods discussing Béatrice. Édouard and Josée walked arm-in-arm up and down the avenues, while Jacques explored the undergrowth, threw pine cones, and returned from time to time to say that what Béatrice needed was a good beating. Josée laughed and Édouard felt somewhat comforted. He ended by admitting that he was short of money and she told him not to worry.

'What I need most I think are friends,' said Édouard, blushing.

Jacques, who joined them just then, said that as far as he was concerned, the friendship was sealed. Josée agreed. From now on they would spend their evenings together. They felt friendly, young, and fairly happy.

Although being with them every day was a great comfort to Édouard, in a way it made him more miserable. After hearing the story of his relationship with Béatrice, they diagnosed that all was lost for him. But he was not so sure. He sometimes saw her between rehearsals, and according to her mood, she either kissed him tenderly and called him 'my love', or did not look at him at all and seemed irritated.

One day he made up his mind to find out where he stood with Béatrice. He met her in a café opposite the theatre. She was more beautiful than ever because she looked pale and tired, which gave her that tragic and noble expression he loved so much. She was in one of her absent-minded moods. He would have preferred to find her more affectionate, so that he would have a chance of hearing her say: 'But of course I love you.' Nevertheless he made up his mind to speak to her:

'How is the play going?'

'I shall have to rehearse all the summer,' she said.

She was in a hurry to go. Jolyet was coming to see the rehearsal. She still did not know if he loved her or whether he looked upon her as just another actress.

'I must ask you something,' said Édouard.

He bent his head and she saw the roots of his fine hair that she had once liked to stroke. She was now completely indifferent to him.

'I love you,' he said, averting his eyes. 'I am afraid you don't love me, or rather, that you no longer love me.' He longed passionately to have this doubt removed. Was it possible, after those nights, her sighs, her laughter ... She did not answer but gazed at a point above his head.

'Answer me,' he said at last. He could not bear it. If only she would speak! He clenched his hands under the table. She seemed to come out of a dream. She was thinking: 'What a bore this is!'

'My dear Édouard, you must realize that I don't love you any more, although I'm still very fond of you. But I *did* love you very much.'

She noted the importance of the words 'very much' in describing her feelings. Édouard raised his head.

'I don't believe you,' he said sadly.

They looked into each other's eyes. This was something they had very rarely done. She had a longing to say: 'I have never loved you – and what about it? Why should I have loved you? Why must one love anybody? Do you think I have nothing better to do?' She thought of the stage at the theatre, sometimes blindingly lit by the footlights, sometimes impenetrably dark, and a wave of happiness swept over her.

'Well, even if you don't believe me,' she continued, 'I'll always be your friend, whatever happens. You are a delightful person, Édouard.'

He interrupted in a low voice:

'But those nights . . .?'

'What do you mean, "those nights"? You . . .' She stopped. He had already gone.

He wandered about the streets like a madman, calling her name, and he felt like knocking his head against a wall. He hated her, he loved her. The memory of their first night together made him almost lose his equilibrium. He walked for a long time, then went to Josée's flat. She forced him to sit down and without a word gave him a strong drink. Édouard went to sleep at once. By the time he woke up Jacques had returned. They all three went out, and later that night returned to the flat, drunk, where they made up a bed for Édouard in the spare room. He stayed with them until the summer.

In June he still loved Béatrice, and, like Alain,

turned first to the theatre page when he opened a newspaper. Summer had descended very suddenly on Paris. To those who had been following the subterranean course of their own passions or inclinations, the hot June sunshine arrived as a shock. It was time to go away, make a break, or add some meaning to the past winter. Everyone hoped to recapture the pleasures of liberty or solitude that come with the thought of holidays, and wondered how, or with whom, they would be spent. Only Béatrice, who was busy rehearsing, was saved from facing the problem. Alain Maligrasse was drinking heavily and Béatrice was now only the pretext for his folly. He had got into the habit of saying: 'I have a job I like, a charming wife, and an agreeable life. So what is wrong?' Nobody seemed able to answer his question. Jolyet had merely remarked that he had taken a long time to find this formula, but that of course it was never too late to take to drink.

Now that Alain had drifted into this form of disorder, he tried to remedy it by the sort of treatment usually resorted to by much younger men – women and alcohol. The trouble with violent, precocious passions, like literature, is that they end by involving one in a lesser kind of evil, which is even more insidious because it comes late in life.

Alain gave himself up to this existence, thinking he had found in it a way to peace and comfort. His life resolved itself into a series of frantic nights with Jacqueline who now went so far as to make jealous scenes, which delighted him, and of days spent in a state of semi-coma.

'I am like Baudelaire's Stranger,' he told Bernard, 'I gaze at the clouds, the marvellous clouds.'

Bernard might have understood that Alain cared for Jacqueline, but not that he liked that kind of life. Besides, he felt slightly envious. He, too, would have liked to drink so as to forget Josée. But he knew very well that he could not escape from himself. One afternoon he had to go and see Fanny and was surprised to find that she had become thinner and was very much on the defensive. Naturally they spoke of Alain, since his addiction to drink was no longer a secret. Bernard had taken over his work at the office and so far Alain had not been asked to leave.

'Can I do anything to help?' asked Bernard.

'Nothing at all,' answered Fanny calmly. 'There was a side of him that I knew nothing about, and which was probably unknown to him as well. Fancy two people living together for twenty years and knowing so little of each other . . .' She made a sad little grimace which touched Bernard. He took her hand and was surprised how quickly she withdrew it, and how vividly she blushed.

'Alain is passing through a crisis,' he said, 'it is nothing very serious.'

'It was all on account of Béatrice. She made him feel that his life was empty . . . yes, I realize it very well. I'm an understanding wife, you see . . .' she said wearily.

Bernard thought of Alain's enthusiastic description of his new life, the significance he attached to the sordid scenes that took place in the bar near the Madeleine.

Bernard kissed Fanny's hand and left. On the stairs he met Édouard who was evidently on his way to see Fanny. Édouard and she never referred to their night together. She had merely thanked him quite naturally for the flowers. He sat at her feet. Looking through the french window at the glorious June sunset, they talked vaguely and sadly about life and about the countryside, which increased Fanny's recent foreboding of impending disaster. Édouard was soothed by a diffused sadness and an embarrassment which was strong enough to bring him back to her every three days, to make sure that he had not made her unhappy. He would return with relief, and almost a feeling of gaiety, to Josée's flat to find Jacques there, madly anxious about the examination he had just taken, and Josée looking over the map of Sweden where they were all three going for their holiday at the end of June.

They all went away as arranged. The Maligrasses were invited to spend a month with friends in the country. Alain drank all the time. Bernard was the only one to remain in Paris. He worked at his novel while Nicole stayed with her parents. As for Béatrice, she interrupted her rehearsals to join her mother on the Riviera where she made several conquests.

Bernard's footsteps echoed on the empty pavements of Paris. There was the seat on which he had kissed Josée for the last time; there was the bar where he had telephoned to her on that awful night when she was not alone; here he had stood, bathed in happiness, on the evening of their return from Poitiers, when he still thought he had something to cling to.

His office looked dusty in the sunshine. He read a great deal and there were now strangely calm moments in the midst of his obsession. Often a view of Poitiers in the rain veiled the reality of Paris in the sun. He walked towards the golden bridges with his regrets and the memories of his regrets. In September the others returned. He caught sight of Josée at the wheel of her car and she pulled up alongside the pavement to speak to him. He leaned through the car window, looking at her thin sunburnt face under the thick black hair, and thought that he would never get over it.

'The trip went off very well. Sweden was beautiful. Édouard drove the car into a ditch, but it was not serious because Jacques . . .'

He could not restrain an angry gesture:

'Excuse my being rather rude, but I think quiet, simple happiness suits you very badly.'

She did not reply, but smiled sadly.

'Forgive me,' he said, 'I'm not in a position to talk of quiet happiness; besides, I have not forgotten that I owe you the only happiness I have had this year.'

She placed her hand on his. They both noticed, without saying anything, that their hands were the same shape. She left and he went home. His sadness made him kind and gentle towards Nicole and she was happy in consequence. It was always like that.

*

'Béatrice, it is your cue.' Béatrice emerged from the dark wings on to the brilliantly lit stage and held out her arms.

'It's not surprising that she is so empty,' thought Jolyet, 'she has all that space, all that silence to fill every day, one cannot ask more of her.'

'I say, she's magnificent!'

The journalist beside him had his eyes fixed on Béatrice. They were in the last days of rehearsal and Jolyet already knew that Béatrice was going to be the sensation of the year and perhaps also a great actress.

'Can you give me a few details about her?'

'She'll provide them herself, my dear fellow, I'm only the producer here.'

The journalist smiled. The whole of Paris knew of their liaison because Jolyet took Béatrice about everywhere. However, he was waiting for the dress rehearsal before 'legalizing' their relationship, much to Béatrice's annoyance. She thought it was healthier to have a lover. If Jolyet had not already compromised her she would have hated him.

'How did you first meet her?'

'She will tell you, she's a very good talker.'

Béatrice was wonderful with the Press. She answered questions with a mixture of amiability and aloofness, which struck exactly the right note for an actress. Luckily she was not yet known, had never been in films, and there was no scandal associated with her name.

She came towards them smiling. Jolyet introduced her to the journalist.

'I'll leave you two together, Béatrice. I'll wait for you downstairs in the bar.'

As Jolyet left, Béatrice followed him with her eyes in a long look aimed at revealing to the reporter what he already knew. Then she turned to him. Half an hour later she joined Jolyet who was drinking a gin fizz, clapped her hands in approval of his choice, and ordered one for herself, which she drank through a straw, raising her big dark eyes to him from time to time.

Jolyet was touched. He found her very sweet with her little tricks and her great ambitions. He thought how strange was this determination to succeed in the great circus of life. He felt conscious of his own cynical outlook.

'How vain all our little efforts seem, dear Béatrice . . .' He began a long speech. One of his favourite diversions was to explain something to her at great length. She would listen attentively and then sum it all up in one wonderfully simple sentence in order to show him she had understood. 'After all,' he thought, 'if she can put it so neatly, it means that I should have been able to do so myself,' and as always when his own mediocrity was brought home to him, he felt a fierce sort of pleasure.

'How true it is,' she answered at last, 'we don't

amount to much. Fortunately we are often un-
aware of it, or we would not attempt anything at
all.'

'That's right,' said Jolyet delightedly. 'Béatrice,
you are perfect!'

He kissed her hand. She made up her mind to
put his intentions to the test. Did he want her, or
was he a homosexual? She did not know of any
other alternative for a man.

'André, do you realize that there are all sorts
of rumours about you? I'm telling you this as a
friend.'

'Rumours about what?'

'About,' she lowered her voice, 'about your
morals.'

He burst out laughing.

'And you believe them? My dear Béatrice, how
can I convince you?'

She knew he was making fun of her. They
stared at each other, and he raised his hand as if
warding off an attack:

'You are very beautiful and very desirable. I
hope you will soon allow me to prove it to you.'

With a regal gesture she held out her hand and
he placed his smiling lips upon it. Decidedly he
adored his profession.

TEN

THE night of the dress rehearsal arrived at last. In her dressing-room Béatrice was looking into the mirror at the stranger in a brocade dress who was going to decide her fate. The dull murmur of voices from the auditorium reached her ears, but she felt quite unmoved. The expected stage-fright had not materialized, although she knew that all good actors experienced it. As she stood contemplating herself she mechanically repeated her first lines:

'Is he here again? Surely it is sufficient that I have obtained his pardon?'

Nothing happened; but her hands felt damp and she had the feeling that the whole situation was absurd. At last she had reached the moment for which she had struggled so long and had thought so much about. She must succeed. She pulled herself together and pinned back a lock of hair.

'You look wonderful!'

Jolyet in a dinner-jacket stood smiling at her in the doorway. He came nearer:

'What a pity we have a duty to perform here. I would have taken you dancing.'

'A duty!' Through the open door she could hear the hum of voices and suddenly realized 'they' were waiting for her, would be talking about her, and she would be the focus of all those eyes. She was frightened, and taking Jolyet's hand, she squeezed it. He was her accomplice, but he was about to abandon her. For a moment she hated him.

'We must go down,' he said.

He had planned the first scene so that as the curtain rose she would have her back to the audience. She was to lean on the piano and only turn round after the actor with her had spoken his second sentence. Jolyet had reasons for this: he would be in the wings where he could watch the expression of her face as the curtain rose behind her. This interested him more than the success of the play. What would Béatrice's instinct prompt her to do? He placed her at the piano and took up his position. The usual three knocks were heard, the curtain rose. She stared fixedly at a pleat in the drapery covering the foot of the piano. Now 'they' could see her. She put out her hand, smoothed a pleat. Then it seemed to her that someone, not herself, turned round:

'Is he here again? Surely it is sufficient that I have obtained his pardon?'

It was over. She went through the scene forgetting that the actor coming towards her was a deadly enemy because his role was as important as hers and also that he was a homosexual. She was going to charm him, to fall in love with him, his was the face of love. She was no longer aware of the dark, breathing mass of people in the theatre. At last she was really alive.

Jolyet had seen the incident of the drapery. He had a sudden premonition that one day Béatrice would make him suffer. During the applause at the end of the first act she went over to him, unmoved and on the defensive. He could not help smiling.

It was a triumph. Josée was enchanted, she had always felt an amused sympathy for Béatrice. Édouard was sitting on her right and she gave him a questioning look. He did not seem particularly impressed.

'It's not bad,' said Jacques, 'but I definitely prefer the cinema.'

Josée smiled at him. He took her hand, and although she detested demonstrations in public, she did not withdraw it. They had not seen each other for a fortnight because she had been to visit her parents in Morocco. That afternoon they had met, after Jacques' lectures, at a friend's house. It was very mild and from the open french window where Josée was sitting she saw Jacques throw down his coat in the hall before hurrying into the room. She did not move but felt an irrepressible smile on her lips. He stood still a moment when he saw her, with the same almost painful smile on his face. She knew, in spite of his being clumsy, head-strong, and rather stupid, that she loved him. While he gave her a quick embrace, because there were others in the room, she had run her fingers through his red hair with no other thought than: 'I love him and he loves me, it's unbelievable!' Since that moment she had hardly dared to breathe.

'Alain seems on the point of going to sleep,' said Édouard.

Maligrasse, who had not seen Béatrice for three months, had arrived at the theatre in a fever of anxiety, but now he felt stone cold. The beautiful stranger who was giving such a splendid per-formance on the stage had nothing to do with him any more. His one idea was to get to the bar as soon as the curtain fell. He longed for a drink. Bernard had been sensible enough to take him out for a whisky in the first interval, but during the second one he had not dared to move. Fanny had made no comment, but he could guess what she was thinking. Now the lights were being dimmed once more. He breathed a sigh of relief.

*

It was wonderful. Everyone had told her so. She knew it herself. But this knowledge was of no use to her. Tomorrow perhaps she would wake up with those words on her lips, and know for certain that she was indeed Béatrice B., the success of the year. But what of tonight? She glanced at Jolyet who was taking her home. He drove slowly and seemed to be thinking.

'How does it feel to be a success?'

She did not reply. Success was the number of curious glances cast in her direction during the dinner which followed the dress rehearsal, the number of exaggerated compliments from people she knew, the number of questions asked. Success was like a victory, something had been won, and she was surprised that the effects should so soon have vanished.

'May I come up?'

Jolyet opened the door for her. She was dead tired, but did not dare to refuse. All this was probably quite logical, but she could not grasp the connexion between the driving force of ambition which had left her no peace since her earliest childhood and the evening which had crowned it.

From her bed she watched Jolyet, in shirt-sleeves, walking up and down the room. He was discussing the play. It was typical of him to become interested in the subject of a play after having chosen it, produced it, and listened to rehearsals for three months.

'I'm extremely thirsty,' he said at last.

She pointed to the kitchen and as he went out of the room, observed his narrow shoulders and his rather too vivacious manner. For a moment she thought with regret of Édouard's long, sinewy body. She would have liked him to be there, or for that matter anyone else, provided he were young and they could go into raptures together over the performance or else joke about it. Someone who would put some life into it all. But there was only Jolyet with his ironical comments, and she must spend the night with him. Her eyes filled with tears; she suddenly felt defenceless and very young. Tears ran down her face while she tried to tell herself that all this was wonderful. Jolyet came back. Fortunately Béatrice knew how to cry without spoiling her looks.

In the middle of the night she woke up and at

once thought of the dress rehearsal, but the memory of her success was not bound up with it. She thought of the three minutes after the curtain had gone up, and of how she had turned round, overcoming some tremendous obstacle by this simple movement of her body. Those three minutes would be hers every evening from now on, and she already felt in a confused way that they would be the only reality in her life; this was to be her fate. Then she went peacefully off to sleep again.

ELEVEN

THE following Monday the Maligrasses gave one of their usual 'evenings', the first since the spring. Bernard and Nicole, Béatrice, modestly triumphant, Édouard, Jacques, and Josée were all there. It was a very gay evening. Alain was a little unsteady, but no one took any notice.

At one moment Bernard found himself leaning against the wall beside Josée where they could watch the others. Just as he was about to ask her a question, she pointed with her chin to Fanny's protégé, the young musician who was just sitting down to play the piano.

'I know that music,' whispered Josée, 'it is very beautiful.'

'It's the same thing he played last year. Do you remember, we were all here and he played that same piece? I suppose he has had no new ideas; the same applies to us, by the way.'

She did not answer, but looked at Jacques, who was at the other side of the room.

Bernard followed her eyes.

'One day you won't love him any more,' he said in a low voice, 'and one day, no doubt, I shall no longer love you. And once again we shall be alone and everything will be the same. And another year will have gone by ...'

'I know,' she said.

In the half-light she took his hand and pressed it, without turning her eyes towards him.

'Josée,' he said, 'what have we been doing all this time? What is the meaning of it all?'

'We must not begin to think in that way,' she said tenderly, 'it will make us mad.'

Other Penguins by Françoise Sagan

BONJOUR TRISTESSE

When her father plans to remarry Cecile sets out to prevent this change in their carefree way of living.

A CERTAIN SMILE

A young girl finds herself in a dilemma when she falls out of love with her student friend and into an entanglement with his uncle.

AIMEZ-VOUS BRAHMS . . .

At thirty-nine a Parisian career girl slides out of a long-lasting affair with a contemporary into an involvement with an Adonis of twenty-five.

Also published

LA CHAMADE

THE HEART-KEEPER

SUNLIGHT ON COLD WATER